MAZE

The

Ballerina

Series

Book 2

BY

URSULA SINCLAIR

First e-book edition 2013 Isisindc Publishing, LLC
Lavernethompson.com
isisindc@msn.com

Editor- Lara Parker
Cover illustration by Dee Allen
Deeallencoverart.com
Cover Model- Colin Wayne
http://colinwayne.com

Photographer- FuriousFotog
http://onefuriousfotog.com

ISBN- 978-0-9859646-5-8 print
ISBN- 978-0-9859646-4-1 eprint

DEDICATION

To all those who take the time and make the effort to perfect a craft you love. Those of us who benefit from your devotion thank you.

Acknowledgements

To my beta readers Derna and Whairigail, thank you for taking the time to make sure I got it right. And to my editor Lara, you always go above and beyond. And next time you'll have more than a 48 hour turn around time. But I'm not promising. Lastly to Alex Cook for showing me the darkness.

The Future

Maze

Have you ever killed anyone?

My breathing remained steady, my heart rate even, but the chemical rush from the adrenaline had blood rushing to my head. The sound of our blades gliding off each other was not a silent one, but the thunder and lightning ensured no one would hear or be inclined to venture out into the downpour this night. We were hemmed in on both sides by the brick walls of the buildings, with just enough room to maneuver. The filthy alleyway only wide enough for a dump truck was made even worse by the torrent of water washing over the soiled ground. Nothing could clear the stench of death creeping around us.

I'd deliberately chosen the time and this place for the confrontation. This was a blind alleyway only one way in and one way out. Barely visible from the street and there were no windows on the sides of the buildings. Just one door from the back of the restaurant near the dumpster. On a night like this, the weather also helped, we would be uninterrupted. No one would step out for a smoke. But at the end of the night, the trash at the restaurant still had to go out.

Huge fat drops of rain poured down from the heavens beating at me, soaking through the clothes I wore. Trying to drive me away from the course I'd set. I ignored it. My body was ready, waiting, my mind bent on one course. It was too late for any other.

The iron door opened to the right of the dumpster I hid beside, and my breath paused for a moment—only one person could be behind it.

I moved silently out from the shadows. As soon as he saw me, he dropped the trash bags he carried and pulled a knife from his boot. He knew damn well why I was there. I stepped toward him, compensating for the slippery ground with my treaded boots but also my balance. I'd trained on many different terrains so the flat alleyway posed no issue for me, but I couldn't say the same about my opponent. He'd already revealed his weakness to me by his crouching stance. His balance would be off if he lunged on such a slick surface.

My body ran cold at what I was about to do. I raised my own blade and beckoned him forward. The glow from the outdoor lighting reflected in his dark hate-filled eyes. We were about the same height and build and our goals were the same. But from there we differed. Jai fought better than he ever had or ever would again because he knew this time he battled for his life. As did I. But as my knife parried and slashed opening flesh, I also fought to protect the one I loved.

So have I ever killed anyone?

I walked away from the alley with that thought in my head, my heart still beat, my blood still ran steadily within my veins. With each step the water turned redder on the ground in front of me. Up until that moment my answer would have been no, I'd never killed anyone. I knew I was capable of it. I'd been trained in the different ways to take a life with my body and weapons since the age of three. I also knew how to put someone down without serious injury. That's what I'd always done. But that was my past. Tonight I'd taken a life to protect those I loved but also out of vengeance. Oh yes, there's hate in my heart, but there's blood on my hands now too. While the rain might have washed the blade of blood, no amount of rainwater would ever wash me clean. Not even the tears I shed could cleanse my soul.

I used the shadows in the alley to make my escape. No one saw me, yet my message was clear for those it was meant for. The Triad wanted to bring on the dragon. Well, he was here, and once let loose, there's no retaining, no stopping. I feared the killing wasn't over. Not until I knew Ivy was safe. Even if it's only from myself. Because how would I face her when this was over? My body remained cold at the thought. But at least she'd be alive.

Chapter One

Present

Ivy

Have you ever heard the sound of a knife slicing through human flesh? It makes a distinct noise I couldn't get out of my head. Not even the roar of the crowd was capable of drowning it from my mind. And the sight.

I'd never seen anything more barbaric. The fight before was nothing compared to this, like a leisurely waltz to the mumbo. The fighters came together like gladiators. They met in the middle of the stage, and engaged. One sword held high the other lower, then sparks flared when the blades clashed. Sliding off the edge of the other, both men spun away disengaging, then came together, arms lifted and swords high to connect again. Four shafts of steel moved in a blur before my eyes. One held in each hand, aimed first in one direction then another in a seemingly chaotic manner but I knew each swing had been calculated. It was hard, even for me, to follow the ebb and flow of their movements. They happened so fast. The fighters' feet moved in perfect synchronicity to their hands. No part of their bodies remained still. Their grunts, soft battle cries and the music of steel provided the tempo. Barbaric? Yes, but artistry, beauty even existed in this. The duo danced; a very intimate intricate dance that could end in death. The ultimate pas de deux. Where only one of them walked away.

I squeezed my eyes shut in a pointless attempt to stop what happened next, as well as my tears. When the sword moved, for a moment, I thought I'd lost my own life. But shutting my eyes stopped nothing. In helpless dread, I watched the opposing fighter swing in an arch that should have opened up Maze's guts and spilled them at his feet. My body shuddered, desperate not to relive that moment, the absolute fear my love would die before my eyes. But even hidden behind my closed eyelids I could still see Maze standing there, awaiting death. Then in a blink, he ducked and then straightened, slicing his blades across the man's knees. Blood flew everywhere. Some of it splashed on Maze. My eyes never left him. His chest rose and fell, his skin covered in sweat and dots of blood. Though the latter wasn't his. Thank you, God. It wasn't his.

After the turnabout, I thought his gaze locked on to me. I couldn't really tell because the tears blocked my vision. I leaped to my feet in horror at what I'd just witnessed, but through it all, I could see Maze standing tall and proud. His swords at his sides. And God help me, I was glad his blood didn't drip upon the floor. Maze had not fallen. *Was that wrong of me?* Knowing he'd just hurt someone to save his own life. I don't know. But I couldn't stop the tears of joy from leaking out.

I tried shutting my eyes tighter to block out the images replaying in an endless loop in my thoughts and tried to keep my breathing even. I told my mind to keep my body relaxed so Maze, who now lay in bed beside me, would not know of my distress.

After the fight he'd come to me, somersaulted over the heads of the crowd to land in front of me, to whisper those three little words. Words that I'd been longing to hear from him. "I love you." Words that were more than sound but emotions lying deep within every part of me for this man. Yet I found when he spoke them, I couldn't just then return the words to him. How could I think of love after witnessing such a barbaric act? Stupid I know.

He could have died and I would have been witness to it. I could do nothing in the moment but wrap my arms around his neck and kiss him. Even that was short lived. Maze's uncle and his bodyguards wasted no time getting us all out of that place. Maze circled his arms around me, not letting me go. The feeling was mutual. I snaked my arm around his waist and I wasn't budging. Someone threw a robe around Maze. We left through a rear exit and all plied into the limo, waiting on the other side of the door, Dante included.

Once in the car, I knew Dante and Mr. Tsang spoke and Maze answered but nothing registered other than the warm body next to mine. We were taken straight back to Maze's uncle's condo. Hours later we were still there but Tsang and his bodyguards had long since departed and Dante had returned home.

I smiled remembering the only thing I could smile about tonight. After Maze had taken a shower and changed, he'd returned to the living room, Dante had stood up and shaken his hand. It was funny to watch them together like that. Dante's blond green-eyed pale looks in contrast to Maze's brown hair, gray eyes and inked skin. But they were a feast for my eyes. It seemed two of my favorite people in the world had made peace. That was the only thing I could smile about right now. Not even afterwards when Maze made love to me and told me he loved me again. I couldn't even manage to say the same once again. Like an idiot all I could do was kiss him, trying to tell him without the words, I loved him too. I wasn't sure what stopped me from saying them out loud. I just knew the phrase wouldn't come.

I felt his arms tighten around me, pulling me closer to him, his warmth, his heat, his fire. Drawing me away from my bleak thoughts of the last few hours. I took a deep breath and wiped the tears from my face in an effort to hide them from him.

Too late.

He turned me so I lay on my back and raised himself up on his elbow to look down at me. It was dark outside, but there was enough ambient light from the streetlights near the windows to filter into the room for him to see the evidence of my tears. He kissed my eyelids, then my mouth.

"God, Ivy, please don't cry. I can't take your tears. What's wrong? Is this because of the fight or because I told you I love you?"

My heart clenched and I cried even harder. He held me tighter in his arms, and helplessly I embraced him. It dawned on me. I could have lost him tonight. When I finally calmed down enough that I thought I could speak, I told him so. "I can't lose anyone else I care about," I whispered against his collarbone. I'd already lost my best friend Shelly in a stupid accident. I refused to lose Maze just because he chose such a dangerous way to live his life.

He kissed my forehead. "You won't lose me."

"How can you say that? After what I saw tonight…" I shook my head. The terror of the night still held me in its grip. "I can't do that again, Maze. I just can't. You could have died tonight." The scene from hours ago flashed once again across my consciousness. I didn't think I'd lose the visions anytime soon. I was sure Maze had crippled the man, but the guy would have killed him. I shuddered.

Maze sighed and leaned away from me. He raised his hand and brushed the hair away from my face, before giving me a quick kiss. "And you won't have to," he said.

"What does that mean?"

"That was my last fight. I'm retiring."

At last, the weight sitting on my chest from the time Maze stepped onto that stage dissolved. Like the words to the song that had been on the radio a moment ago, Maze's words blew it away.

"You are? Are you sure?" Why did I say that? I didn't want him to fight anymore. I didn't want him to risk his life or his limbs. I wanted him safe, whole. I wanted him with me. But it was selfish. I knew how much his sport meant to him, as much as dance did to me. I might be forced to give up something I've lived for and worked toward all my life. How could I ask him to give up what he did? I wasn't sure what the right thing to do was for either of us. But if he wanted to retire, I wasn't going to talk him out of it. Was that selfish? Yes, but I had no problem with that if it meant he would be safe.

"Yes, I am," he said. "I'm going to begin training the next round of fighters at the gym where I've been working out. Uncle Tsang owns it, and tonight, he signed the building and the business over to me."

"What!"

He just smiled.

"So is that why only you and your uncle went into the den? This was the quick business he had to discuss with you?" After Maze and Dante had made peace, Tsang had taken Maze aside. They hadn't been gone long. But Dante only wanted to talk about how badass my boyfriend was. I only wanted to forget. "Did you know about this before... Before the fight?" I questioned.

"No. I was shocked he'd do such a thing. But in truth not surprised. He's always looked out for me."

I smiled but tears continued to roll down my face. They were happy ones this time. "So this is legit? No more of these dangerous fights? You won't need a bodyguard or anything like your uncle?"

He smiled and shook his head, while rubbing my tears away. "No more fights. And I've never needed a bodyguard."

I wasn't an idiot, but I guessed his uncle's business dealings weren't quite legit and neither were these fights. I needed to know this venture he was entering was real though.

"No more violence like what I saw tonight?" I'd asked.

"Well I'd still get into the ring but as a trainer, no more professional fights. That was my last one."

I blinked and grinned. "So this is real?"

He leaned forward and kissed my forehead. "As real as that. Now please, for me, stop crying. Everything will be fine." He wiped the remaining tears off my face with his thumb.

"Maze." I sat up and turned until I was on my knees beside him, kissing him all over his face. "I lo— Care about you so much. I just couldn't… I can't watch you get hurt."

"Never again, babe. I promise."

I had to let my fear go. I had to trust him. Trust us. There was only one thing, well, maybe two left to do. I raised my hands and placed them on either side of his beautiful face, looked into his swirling storm-colored eyes. I could have lost him forever tonight. I found what I searched for in the depths of his gaze, and gave him the words he needed from me.

"I love you."

He smiled and lightning seemed to flash in his orbs. "And I you," he said before placing his mouth over mine, claiming me again as only he could. His body covered mine, and I opened myself up to him, spreading my legs for him. It was only a little while before he filled me; his entry took my breath away. Wrapped in his arms, his love consumed me. I raised my legs and clamped them around his waist so he could go deeper. He didn't disappoint, and if I could carry him safe inside me always I would.

Chapter Two

Maze

Vague, blurry images of my mom flashed across my mind. They were the only memories really I had of her. I looked at pictures of her and I could see I'd inherited some of her features. My hair and eye color. But I had no clear recollection of what she looked like other than the photographs. What I recalled most was her scent, like a combination of vanilla and something flowery, and the melody to her favorite song. *Dust in the Wind.* She'd play it over and over while she danced with me in her arms. Then I remembered one day those arms just being gone and the sound of a child screaming in despair. But most of all I remembered her incredible love for me. Kinda the way I loved the woman who lay beside me. *Ivy.* My world.

After my uncle and Dante had departed, I'd turned on the radio in the master bedroom and left it on low. The music pulling at me was a song from my childhood that brought me out of a deep satisfied sleep. That and Ivy's stiffness, her ragged breathing. My baby was hurting, and she tried to hide it from me. Damn. I knew in my soul I shouldn't have ever let her see me fight like that. Knew in my heart the raw savagery would be too much for her, but she wanted to be there and I couldn't deny her anything. I'd denied us both so much already. In truth, I needed her there as much as I think she needed to be there. It was over now. All over. Uncle Tsang and Joe made sure I had no choice but to win. And even though the choice wasn't mine to stop fighting, it was the right thing to do. The Triad wouldn't tolerate what I'd done. They'd be out for my blood if I ever tried to fight pro again. They still might despite the fact I'd retired.

I knew Tsang and his bodyguards hustled us out of the arena in order to prevent any immediate retaliation. Even now Tsang and Joe had taken steps to protect me as well as the Tong, the legitimate business association Joe had built. I wasn't stupid. All of this I understood they'd do. It was the reason we had come back to the condo. Tsang owned the entire building, and most of the businesses on the block owed him. No one could touch us here. I was floored when he offered me ownership of his gym outright. No strings attached. I could build the place as I saw fit. He had the paperwork ready to go. Everything was already filled out.

They just needed my signature. I didn't know Joe had a small interest in the gym too until I saw the names on the document. His signature written next to Uncle Tsang. They signed all of their interest over to me. Both the deed and gym were placed in my name. I just had to stop fighting. It was a difficult decision for me to step down. Even though I really had little choice, I did it willingly. There was also Ivy to consider. My heart. My soul. My reason for being. And right now she was hurting.

I understood why and I knew how to relieve her fears.

I turned her over. She couldn't hide those tears from me. I told her what she needed to hear, to finally get everything out in the open. Well, the parts that mattered to her. The look on her face, when I told her I was giving up fighting, was worth everything to me.

My heart damned near wanted to explode when she told me she loved me. Shit. If I didn't know I already loved her I would have known at that moment. She was mine. Always had been. Always would be. And God help any sonofabitch who tried to take her away from me.

I set out to prove to her just how very much I loved her. We'd already made love once tonight. But that was hard and fast, too fast, but at the time it was what we both needed. I understood she had to make sure I was still in this world with her and I needed to be inside her, claim her, brand her like I've never wanted to another. But this time right now was about us. Belonging together, pledging ourselves to each other, truly making love because nothing stood between us now. When she parted her thighs for me and I entered her slick wetness, a sigh of utter pleasure escaped from me. I filled her, wanting to go deeper inside of her. Wanting her to take all of me, as I wanted to become everything to her. I took both of her soft hands into my calloused ones and raised them until they rested beside her head. She threaded her fingers through my own and we stared at each other. I continued to rock in and out of her. Feeling every inch of her upon my skin and letting her into my heart.

She raised her legs and wrapped them around my waist, drowning me. I wanted to make this last for us both. I needed her to know I would always be there for her. I would never leave her or hurt her. "I love you. I will never hurt you again. You are my balance. My light and my heart."

Then I lowered my lips to hers because I couldn't resist joining us there, too. My mouth covered hers and her tongue greeted mine as it entered. I moaned into her and we made love there, too. Blood rushed to my dick swelling it even more, and my balls tightened. Not yet. No. I wanted to stay inside her forever. *Ivy. Mine.*

I pulled away slightly and rolled until she lay on top of me. I yearned to make it last and so I needed to slow down. She sat up on me and lifted herself up and down on my cock. I held her hips loosely letting her set the rhythm. But then her sex muscles clapped around me and I instinctually surged up into her in response.

A strangled curse escaped my lips at her sudden tightness. I must have been crazy to think this position would slow us down. Bullshit! As long as we were joined there was no slowing down. Despite that cast on her foot, my girl rode me like a rodeo bronco. My fingers dug into her hips and she increased her movements. All the while I kept time with her. Her breathing came in quick pants, her flat stomach muscles clenched, and I had to fight not to explode into her. She was so beautiful as she tossed her head back and opened her mouth. Her sex tightened around me just before her heat coated my dick. It was over.

"Fuck!" I had no control over the surge rushing through my body. There was only one outcome. My hips left the bed, taking her with me. My balls tightened, and my essence released inside of her. Still joined, I sat up and helped her straighten her legs over mine to shift the cast as she continued to bear down on me and I continued to cum into her.

Finally, depleted and with our legs entwined and wrapped in each other's arms, we slept. The sound of thunder outside had me tightening my arms around Ivy. I grabbed my cell on the nightstand to check the time. It was going on ten a.m. We'd slept in this morning, but we both needed the rest. When I turned back, Ivy was wide-awake and smiling at me. Damn. I'd already glanced at the windows and saw the day was gray, cloudy, and raining outside. But inside, right here, nothing but pure sunshine reigned. I smiled back at her and moved to kiss her, but her phone on the other side of the bed chimed.

She pushed away from me. "Oh, oh," she said.

"What is it?"

"My folks."

I took the phone then handed it to her.

"Hi, Mom," she said, relaxing back onto the pillow.

I bent my arm at the elbow, placing it under my head as I lay on my side facing her. I ran my fingers along her waist to her thigh, trying to get her to part her legs. She swatted my hand away and grinned.

I smiled, but decided I had to stop teasing her.

I threw off the covers and headed to the bathroom and the shower. Giving her some privacy. I knew she still hadn't told her parents about her accident. And she also hadn't told them a thing about me. Would she tell them now or wait? Not that they'd remember me from all those years ago. I kinda hoped they didn't. I wasn't so sure I made such a good impression back then. And with my background, and all the new artwork running all over my body, I wasn't sure I'd make a great impression now.

At least I don't have any nipple piercings. That was like waving a red flag to a bull in the arena. But my ears were pierced. I just rarely wore anything in them. I wonder how Ivy felt about piercings? I wouldn't do anything to make her uncomfortable. Nor have her parents dislike her choice of a boyfriend. In the end though, it didn't matter what her folks thought of me. As long as Ivy loved me, that's all I cared about. Still, I didn't want them to hate me. I was a part of their daughter's life and I damn sure wasn't going anywhere. Which meant sooner or later they were bound to meet me, and for Ivy, I'd do everything to make sure I didn't cause a problem between her and her folks. If that meant wearing long sleeves to hide my ink, hide it I would.

After brushing my teeth and taking care of business, I turned on the shower and got in. I'd left the bathroom door ajar and lingered a little, hoping Ivy would come join me. But when she didn't, I started to worry a little. Maybe the call with her folks didn't go so well.

I'd just finished drying off when the door pushed all the way open and she stepped in wearing my t-shirt.

She was so goddamned beautiful. All warm brown skin over a sleek toned body. And she was all mine.

I licked my lips wanting to taste her. But when my gaze reached her mouth I saw the tremble. I took the two steps that separated us and got her attention. There were tears in her eyes.

"Babe, what is it? Is something wrong?"

She blinked. "I told my parents about my injury and they were really supportive, but also a little disappointed I hadn't called them right away. They understood I just needed a little time, though."

I was confused. There had to be more to warrant her tears. "Okay."

She lowered her head and then raised it to look at me again. A sheen of tears still in her eyes. "It's…my mom, and Shelly's parents. They're all coming to New York tomorrow."

I nodded still not understanding why this should upset her. She didn't have to explain to me who Shelly was. I knew Shelly. I was there the night she died. Even though we really didn't keep in touch during the almost five years I'd been in Japan. My doing I think. I didn't encourage her to contact me. But I texted her every year on the day of Shelly's death to let her know I still thought of her and wanted to make sure she was okay. I knew what Shelly meant to her.

Ivy seemed hesitant, maybe because she didn't want to hurt my feelings. She wanted to meet with her people alone. Was she ashamed of me or felt she had to hide me from her family? My heart sorta missed a beat at the thought. But I'd do anything for her. If she wanted to keep us a secret, then shit, for now I would be.

Steeling myself for it, I wrapped my arm around her so she wouldn't see the hurt in my eyes. "That's great. Do you...do you want to spend time with them alone? Want me to stay behind?"

Please say no.

She shook her head and her eyes opened wide at my question. "Why would I want to do that? I told my mom we're seeing each other again. She remembered you."

The pain gripping my chest suddenly disappeared but I couldn't smile. Something still wasn't right here. "Then what's making you so sad?"

"Maze...Shelly's mom. Bev, she's been diagnosed with cancer. They're coming here to see a specialist before deciding on the type of surgery she should have."

"Oh, babe. I'm so sorry." I wrapped my arms around her tighter while she cried into my chest. I knew she wasn't just crying for Shelly's mom as much as for her daughter, Ivy's best friend, who'd died so long ago.

I kissed her eyelids then her mouth, hugging her while I did. I just wanted to comfort her, so I gave her what she needed. My love, my arms, my support. They were all hers.

She pulled back. "I'm such a mess. I'd like to use the bathroom and take a shower. I need to get into some clean clothes, too."

"Okay." I stepped back, but put my hands on her arms and nuzzled her neck for a minute. "You go ahead and jump in the shower. How about I run down the street and grab a couple of bagels for us? After we eat, we'll head to your place for you to change. Then I need to run to the hospital. Joe's been moved out of ICU but I want to check on him. You can come with me if you like. Or I'll come back when I'm done and we can decide what to do for the rest of the day. Whatever you want." Yeah. As long as we did it together.

She smiled. "I'd like that. I'll come with you. By the way, do you have a plastic bag around here I can wrap my foot in?"

I looked down at her cast and frowned, understanding

the problem. She couldn't get it wet. "Hang on a sec." I left the bathroom and headed for the kitchen.

I returned with a bag and wrapped her foot. "Need anything else?"

She shook her head. "Thanks. I'm good."

I kissed her quickly and left the bathroom to give her some privacy. I put on the jeans I'd worn to the fight last night, thinking I needed to stop by the brownstone to get a change of clothes, too. I grabbed Ivy's clothes from the floor, and then opened the bathroom door.

"Babe, I'm just putting your clothes on the counter for you and grabbing my shirt."

"Thanks," she said from the shower.

"I'll run and get us breakfast, then I'll be right back." I shut the door behind me and headed for the living room.

I found the keys Uncle Tsang had left on the table the night before then I opened the front door. As soon as I set foot in the hallway, I registered the person in a chair at the end of the hall near the elevator. There were eight units on each floor. The condo was on one side of the building and the elevator at the opposite end of the hallway.

I walked right up to the man who sat on the chair. I recognized his mixed East Asian features. He was one of Tsang's bodyguards, Terry. Even sitting he looked huge; his head came to my chest. He'd been with us last night at the fight. I understood what his presence meant. I was not going to be allowed to just walk away. At least not yet. I'd won a fight I was supposed to lose. Someone was out for blood. I was pissed I needed a shadow. He spoke before I could.

"What do you need, Maze?" He already had his phone out to make the call.

"I just wanted to get a couple of bagels from the corner. Then Ivy and I are heading over to her place. After that the hospital."

He stood. "I'll walk down to the corner with you, and when you're ready to leave, you know the number to call. We'll bring a car around for you."

"Fuck!" I took a deep breath. No use yelling at him. "Do I need a bodyguard?"
He looked at me and tilted his head. "You'll have to ask your uncle. But I'm yours for now."

I knew it was pointless to argue with him. I was his job and he wasn't leaving my side unless I kicked his ass or Uncle Tsang told him to back off. Since I already knew, for now, neither was going to happen, I shrugged. "Shit, fine."

I turned around to stare back down the hall. I couldn't see the door from this angle, but I knew my heart resided in that room. "Is it safe to leave Ivy?"

"The building is secure. No one comes up here who's not supposed to be here."

I nodded. Figures. It's why Tsang insisted we come back here after the fight. I knew that. Tempers were still running high. Always a dangerous time. "Okay. Let's go."

I felt really stupid walking down the street with Terry carrying a damn umbrella over my head. Dude watched everyone on the street. But then again so did I. It was pouring so not a whole lot of people were out and about.

We got to the bagel place and I placed the order. Getting an extra one for Terry. The man didn't even crack a smile when I gave it to him. Just took the bag and said thanks. From the time I left until the time I got back to the condo all of about twenty minutes had gone by. When I pushed the door open the first thing I saw was Ivy standing near the window watching the rain. My heart slammed against my chest. I didn't give a shit what the Triad did or didn't want. Whatever they tried to throw at me. I was not giving her up.

She turned when I walked in and smiled.

"Food," I said coming toward her. "And I grabbed a couple of plain white teas, too."

She met me part of the way and took the bags out of my hands then moved to the small kitchen area. There was no room for a table there, only a breakfast bar with four stools.

She placed the bags on the counter and we sat down while I pulled out what I'd gotten. Two bacon, egg, and cheese bagels for me, one for her, and two cups of tea.

"Sorry, it's a little wet. But it's pouring out there," I said.

"I'm sorry you had to go out in this mess. But thank you for doing it. Did you have to go far?'

"Nope, just down to the end of the block."

"You're not very wet." She frowned. "Did you have an umbrella?"

Trust her to notice. "Ah, no, but I ran into a friend in the hallway who did. He let me borrow his umbrella. I returned it when I got back."

"Oh, good." She took a sip of the tea. "This is good. Just the way I like it. O' natural." She smiled then glanced over at the windows again where we could see the deluge of water falling from the sky. "Do you think we'll be able to get a cab in this?"

"No worries. Uncle Tsang left one of his cars and a driver for us to use."

No way did I want Ivy to see the bodyguards hovering around me for the next few days. It was one of the things I told Terry on our walk. I also told him when I was ready I'd call him for the car, and he was not to be in that hallway when we left. I remained optimistic Uncle Tsang would be able to take care of all of this mess in a few days, and Ivy and I could get on with being a normal couple. Ones who didn't need bodyguards and Ivy didn't have a boyfriend who got into fights while they were out on a date. Besides, if her mom and Shel's mom were coming to town tomorrow, I was the last thing Ivy needed to worry about.

Chapter Three

Ivy

We'd spent most of the day yesterday with Joe and after a quick trip back to the brownstone in Brooklyn. Maze needed a change of clothes, and then we came back to my place. Before we left Maze said, even as corny as it sounded, "Your place or mine?" It made my heart flutter. But just looking at him could do that, too.

My God what did I ever do to deserve him? He was mine. All mine. I did a mental happy dance every time I glanced at him. Six feet two inches of masculine perfection. Gray eyes the color of storm clouds stared at me and all I wanted to do was bathe in them, each and every time he looked my way. And the love shining from those orbs warmed all of me.

We decided my place was closer to the hospital. Joe would be there for some time so it would be easier to get there from my condo. However, Maze having a car at his disposal proved to be a real bonus in regards to a quick means of transportation. I still didn't quite get why his uncle left us his car and driver. Maze told me Mr. Tsang wouldn't need it for the rest of the week and said we could use it. Which was great and thoughtful of him. I didn't have to hobble around on the sidewalk trying to flag down a cab.

I smiled. Between hanging out with Dante, and now Maze, I might never have to worry about catching a cab in New York during rush hour again. But then depression crept into my thoughts as to why I didn't have to worry about my schedule and traffic. Dante had already left for the day for another meeting with the dance company. It would be weeks before my cast was off and months before I could even try to dance again. If ever.

"Don't."

I blinked at the sound of Maze's voice and glanced over at him. I stretched my arms out on the sofa and placed my legs on the coffee table. My cast rested on top of a pillow to make my lounge more comfortable. The television was on. Maze and I were just killing time before we met my mom and Shel's mom later this evening for dinner.

"Thank you for coming with me tonight, baby. I...I don't want to face this alone."

He brushed his finger along my cheekbone. "I'm always here for you. Do you know how the appointment went?"

I sighed. "They confirmed the diagnosis, but the doctors think they caught it in time and everyone's agreed on the surgery."

"That's good then?" Maze asked.

"Yeah, it is."

"We have awhile before we have to leave, do you want something to drink?"

"Thanks. I think there are some snacks too in that first cabinet next to the sink if you're hungry."

Maze stood and went into the kitchen. I watched him walk there and back. He had on black dress slacks and a shiny, cotton long-sleeved dark gray shirt. A black belt with a silver buckle graced his slim hips. He still wore his hair on the short side, but it had that 'I just rolled out of bed' look and all I wanted to do was roll back into bed with him. Damn he was gorgeous. He'd turned me into a nymphomaniac. I couldn't get enough of him. Then again he acted worse than I did.

"You sure you okay, babe?"

I shook my head to stop ogling him. It didn't escape my notice his shirt covered up any exposed tats. He never covered them all up like that. I could only assume he did it for me. For today, when meeting my family.

He held a serving tray in his hands when he returned to

the sofa. After lowering the tray to rest on the coffee table, he grabbed one of the open beers, handing it to me before grabbing the other one and sitting down. He sat next to me, and I leaned my head against his shoulder.

I sighed, he'd momentarily distracted me, but I realized I hadn't responded to his comment. "I'll be fine."

"Yes. You will be. But what were you thinking about?"

I shrugged. "Just everything. My injury. Being able to dance again. Shel. Her mom. You. Me. Us."

"Whoa! You really *were* thinking about everything. Then you should know you have nothing to worry about. At least not about yourself, me, or us. I will do whatever it takes to help you dance again if that's what you want to do. And if you decide you want to do something else, I'm down with that too. There is an *us*. There always has been and always will be. And you and your family will be there for Shel's mom." He kissed my forehead. "And I'll be there for you. So stop worrying."

I smiled, shifting to place my head on his shoulder. "That's definitely an easy thing to say, but I will try."

He threaded his fingers through my hair, and I took comfort in his presence. "Thank you for covering up, but really, you didn't have to do that. I want them to accept you as you are. I love your ink." I rested my hand on his chest.

"Especially the heart wrapped in ivy."

This time, he pressed his lips to mine. "I know. But I don't want them forming any preconceived notions the first, well, second time we meet."

"You know they've already seen some of your tats years ago, right?"

"Yeah, well, hopefully they'll remember my charming personality more."

I grinned but still couldn't quite relax. As good as everything was between us, I couldn't shake the feeling that something seemed a little off. Though, I couldn't exactly put my finger on it. Silly, I know. A lot had happened to me in the last few days and a lot was still going on. The circumstances would drive anyone batty.

I leaned forward to put the beer down and then sat back against Maze. I caressed his chest again; he was hard all over. His heart muscle pushed against his rib cage, the vibration echoing up through his skin to my palm. Yeah, it matched the racing of my heart.

I raised my eyes to see him staring at me, a sexy grin on his face and heat in his gaze. He leaned forward to place his beer next to mine on the coffee table. After he sat back against the couch he shifted us both. He moved one of his legs and had me lean forward so he could place it behind me on the couch. He left his other foot on the floor and positioned me so I could lie between his thighs with my back against his chest.

"Move your left leg and put it up next to mine," he whispered against my ear. "Leave your other on the coffee table."

I did as he asked. Since we were going out soon to dinner I wore a dress, it wasn't exactly short, but it rose up, which left me wide open to him.

Both of his arms snaked around my waist. He drew me farther up until my ass rested against the hardness throbbing and poking at my tailbone. One of his hands pulled my dress up even more, while the other grabbed and squeezed my thigh. When he'd exposed much of my silky black underwear he whispered, his voice low and husky, "I think black's my favorite color."

He moved his hand off my dress and pulled aside my underwear, my wet underwear, so his thumb could brush against my clit.

"You are so wet. I'm going to have to do something about that."

I was already raising my hips to his touch and widening my legs but still I had to at least try to dissuade him. "We don't have much time before we have to leave." Not like I tried very hard given my reaction.

"We've got enough. Besides, we don't have to worry about waiting around for a cab at this hour. Terry will bring the car around as soon as I text."

"Mmm..." I heard what he said but it wasn't really registering because he'd inserted one finger into my sex and I tightened my muscles to hold him in there. I raised my arms over my head to circle them around his neck, while sinking against him. His length flexed against the top of my butt, his strong thigh muscles contracted around my hips, and he shifted. He pressed his sex even more against the top of my ass and I felt how much he wanted me. And I wanted everything he had to give to me.

His lips brushed against my inner arm, then his tongue licked my skin at the same time he stuck two fingers inside me, and between one breath and the next, I shattered.

"You are so fucking responsive," he murmured.

He turned my head and covered my mouth with his, all the while continuously working my sex. His fingers moved in and out, and I moaned into his mouth.

Suddenly he stiffened and withdrew his hand out from between my legs. Without warning, he pulled my dress down to cover me, and I heard the key turn in the lock.

I popped my eyes open. *Dante. Crap!*

Quickly I lowered my arm and placed my leg on the floor but continued to rest against Maze. He wrapped his arms around my waist resting his head on my shoulder.

"We'll finish this later," he whispered just as Dante pushed open the door.

"Hey, wassup?" he said when he saw us. Then he turned and shut and locked the door.

I twisted so I could see him better, but he walked around the couch and took a seat on the chair at the other end of us. He shifted the dance bag he wore across his shoulder and placed it on the floor beside him. He wore dark blue and black dance sweats. We had a matching set.

A wave of sadness hit me to see him in his when I knew it would be a long time before I'd wear mine again.

"Hey, man," Maze said.

Dante looked at us then frowned. I thought perhaps he picked up on my bleak mood but I shrugged off the feeling. I needed to know how the directors had planned out the rest of the year. This was the first chance I had to ask Dante about what was going on with the company. I needed a head's up. Yeah, I could have called Davis, the production director, but frankly he hated talking on the phone. He preferred you set up an appointment with his secretary so he would be prepared to talk. I already scheduled a time to come and talk to him tomorrow through his secretary.

"So how'd the meeting go?" I asked. There'd been a meeting today to discuss the rest of the summer, and the season in greater detail.

He sighed. "I turned in the paperwork you left for me and they took it. So you're officially on the injured list. I know you're talking to them tomorrow but I can tell you right now what they've already told me. They'll hold your spot until August, but then you'll have to show them you're still able to perform to maintain it. I'm sure Davis will also tell you he would like us to put together some chorography for Christy and me but that won't be for awhile. Christy will take the duets, and your solo roles they're going to spread out between Christy, Lisa, and Stephanie, so that's good."

"That is good news. I'd love to do some chorography. I'm not so excited about working with Christy but I'll do it. So why are you still frowning?" I asked. Something in his expression suggested more was going on.

"They're thinking about holding auditions to fill a couple of openings."

"Yes, we knew they were going to do that," I said, but a sinking feeling crept up on me.

"Yeah, but now I think they'll also look to bring on someone that can handle your roles. Someone who can step right in or they can begin to train." Dante placed his hands on his thighs and leaned forward. "And even if you did come back strong they'd still want another ballerina of your caliber they can cultivate in the company. 'Cause let's face it, Christy is no prima ballerina."

"Shit." I was being replaced. Maybe not right away if I overcame my injury, but eventually. It happens to us all. Sooner or later, someone younger, stronger, and better came along. I too had replaced someone else when I was hired. Tessa was no longer with the company. I had taken her place. Just as Dante became the principal male dancer when he nudged Jeffery out of his spot. Although he was still around. We were all replaced sooner or later. Understanding that didn't make it easier, though. A dancer is what I was in my soul. My mood took a nosedive.

"What does this mean?" Maze asked.

I twisted to look at him, doing my best to look content when I was anything but. "I'm being replaced."

"Now, that's not quite true, Ivy," Dante spoke up.

I swung back to face him. "You and I both know if not now then later, but that's what it means. They will have a replacement ready to go."

"But what if you come back good as new?" Maze asked. "Doesn't that make a difference?"

"Yes, it does," I replied. "It means I'd keep my position as the featured female lead for maybe another few seasons, but sooner or later I will be replaced."

"Fucking hell," Maze grunted. "Well they're not replacing you yet. I already promised you I would help. We'll get that ankle so strong you'll be even better on it than you were before."

"You know," Dante said, "I'm kinda liking this guy. Fucking A." He got up and came over to fist bump Maze's hand. "Okay, kiddies, I gotta go take a shower, order a little take out, then go to bed. I have to be at the theatre at six tomorrow to go over the routine with Christy. We're doing a special performance in a couple of days. We're filling in for a duo that had to cancel at the last minute."

"Where's Christy?" I asked. Oops, I didn't mean to say that out loud. I knew Dante hadn't been hanging with her lately, but Christy was very into him. I was sure she just loved the fact they were dancing together. "Sorry, forget I said anything."

"No. It's cool. I told you we're taking a break. She got too clingy and you know me. I like variety. Anyway enjoy the rest of your evening and I'll see you both later."

"Night, man," Maze said.

"Night," I repeated. We were silent as we watched Dante

go into his room then shut his door. "I guess we better go to the restaurant," I stated.

"No matter what you'll be okay," Maze replied, trailing his hand down the side of my face.

My lips trembled but I fought the fog threatened to drag me under. I twisted around to look at him. "Promise?"

"I swear." He raised my hand and kissed it. "I better call the car around or we'll be late."

Chapter Four

Maze

We walked into the restaurant lobby just as the hostess seated Ivy's mom and friends. I would have known Ivy's mother anywhere. Her daughter looked a lot like her. They had the same warm brown coloring and were both about the same height. Her mom probably only weighed a little more than Ivy did. Where Ivy's hair was past her shoulders and wavy, Allison wore her hair cut in a short, capped curly style that worked great with her high cheekbones. The same ones she gave her daughter. Ivy introduced me to all of them. Ivy's mom, who told me to call her Allison, and Shel's parents remembered me, or claimed they did. Both women hugged me, which surprised the hell outta me. Shel's dad, Ben, shook my hand. Since my mother died, I could count the number of times on one hand I was hugged that had nothing to do with a prelude to sex.

It was nice being hugged by the two moms. I didn't want Ivy to know but I was nervous. I wanted to make a good impression on them. I wanted them to know how much I cared about Ivy. She was everything to me and I'd be good to her. I didn't deserve her. I knew that, but damn, if I wasn't going to try and live up to her and her family's expectations. It was clear Ivy and her mother were close. They sat next to each other and chatted, teasing each other the way a mother and daughter could. Ivy's chair sat close to mine and we held hands under the table the entire time. I think her mom knew, though. I caught her looking at our arms one time and then she looked at me and winked. So I guess I didn't come off as a total loser.

The awkward moment came when Ben asked about what I did. I didn't want to lie to these folks. I took a sip of the wine in front of me and manned up.

"I'm a retired mixed martial arts fighter, sir."

"Wow," Ben said. "I've been to one of those fights. Very intense."

"You have?" Bev, his wife, asked.

Ben took a sip of water. "Yes, with Phil."

I remembered, Phil was Ivy's dad. Both moms laughed. "So what was your record?" Ben asked.

Ivy answered before I could. "Undefeated," she said proudly beaming.

I wanted to lean over and kiss her right then and there in

front of her parent and their friends, but I wasn't sure that would be a good idea. It wouldn't have been a quick kiss either. At that moment a rush of love filled me, at the way she took pride in me. I was so busy staring at her I almost missed her mother's next question.

"So what are your plans now?" Allison asked.

I turned my attention away from Ivy to answer it. "I'm the new owner of a martial arts gym over in Chinatown. I'm going to start training the next crop of fighters."

"Nice," Ben said. "So no more cage fighting for you?"

"Oh how exciting," Bev said at the same time.

I shook my head at Ben's statement. "No more fighting. Just training. That will be enough excitement."

"Well, I think this calls for a toast. Congratulations," Allison said.

They all raised their glasses and toasted me. I breathed a sigh of relief that I'd passed that hurdle and been accepted by Ivy's mom and people who meant something to her. The talk then moved to Ivy and her injuries. They were interested in the fact I was willing to help her come back from it.

"Yes," I agreed. "As soon as the cast comes off I'm going to have her down at the gym working on strengthening her ankle."

"I think that's a fantastic idea, Maze," Bev responded.

Dinner turned out much better than I'd thought it would have. When we parted company in front of the restaurant, the hug I got from Allison was a little tighter than when we first got there.

She whispered in my ear, "Thank you."

I just smiled at her and nodded. Then she got into the cab with Shel's parents and I closed the door.

"That went well," I said.

Ivy tilted her head and stared at me. "Were you worried?"

I shrugged. "Scared shitless."

She laughed. "My mom liked you. They all did. You impressed them."

I wrapped my arm around her and drew her against my side just as Terry pulled up to the curb with the limo. "As long as I impress you," I replied, and gave her a quick kiss. I opened the car door for her before Terry could come around the side. "I got it man," I said to our driver and climbed in behind her.

"I'm glad you came with me," she stated.

I clutched her hand. "Yeah, me too."

It wasn't too late and I needed to check on Joe. I wanted to tell him about meeting Ivy's mom. I hoped one day soon he'd be able to meet her parents. I even talked to Allison a little about Joe and she said she'd love to meet him sometime. I'd like him to meet her too, but they were headed back home tomorrow, so it would be a while.

Ivy lay snuggled within the crook of my arm, her hand on my thigh and mine over her hand. I threaded our fingers together. I liked touching her. "I found it interesting as much as we talked at dinner, no one mentioned the reason they were all here. Was it because I was there?"

"No. I think they're just trying not to dwell on it. You being there gave them something else to focus on. Bev will go back home and schedule the surgery."

"Well she looks good. If I didn't know she was ill I wouldn't suspect a thing. Has she any idea of when that will be?

Ivy nodded. "It will be sometime late next week and I think I'll go for a visit then."

This was the first I heard she might be leaving me. Not for awhile, yes, but still. I didn't want to spend even a minute without her being nearby. "How long do you think you'll be gone?"

"Just a few days. I'll go a couple of days before the surgery and if all goes well come back the day after. You could come with me."

"Babe, I'd love to, but tomorrow I have to meet with

Tsang and a few of the managers who use the gym. We're going to plan out some renovations for the place. That might start as early as next week so I'm not sure. But thank you for asking and wanting me to be there with you. I want to be. Maybe I can fly down and be with you for the surgery then fly back the next day or something." But I already knew come hell or high water I'd be there with Ivy at least for the surgery. "As soon as you know the date let me know and I'll make sure whatever is being delivered or installed will be done around those two days so I can be there with you. How's that?"

She gazed at him with her heart in her eyes. "Have I told you today I love you?"

I smirked. "I don't remember so why don't you remind me?"

"I love you."

I shook my head. "Not even close to how much I love you." I took her into my arms and closed my mouth over hers. You know I'd always known I had the capacity for this kind of love. I'd known it for several years. The thing was it was only and always for just one person. I held her in my arms and I'd do whatever it took to keep her there.

****

The car pulled up to the hospital entrance and I helped

Ivy out. Terry drove it around to a parking area and would wait there for us. I just had to call or text him when I was ready.

We'd just walked through the admittance area when the hairs at the base of my neck stood up. Someone was watching us and it wasn't friendly-like. I slowed my steps and glanced around, quickly spotting the buzz cut of one of Jai's buddy's from the alley that night in Little Italy. When the dude looked at me and nodded, I knew it was no accident he sat there in the hospital. He'd been waiting on me. *Shit!* Those fuckers were too close to Joe, but at least I knew they couldn't get to him. Only family was allowed to see him and those on a guest list. Uncle Tsang told me last night he'd taken care of that. Along with placing a guard outside Joe's door. No one could get to my stepfather in the hospital. So he had to be there for me.

"Ivy, I see someone I need to speak to for a minute to let them know they can't see Joe. Will you go on up, and I'll met you there?"

She turned to me. Her forehead crinkled and her lips flatted out into a frown. "I'll wait for you."

"No. It's okay, thanks, but you go on up. I'll be right behind you."

Even though I didn't believe she'd seen whom I'd been

staring at, she still looked around. There were quite a few folks in the waiting area, I hoped that night in the alley it was too dark and she was too scared to remember what the men looked like. Thankfully, her gaze went past the guy. Finally, she looked at me again and appeared thoughtful before replying. "All right."

I gave her the room number and squeezed her hand before she walked away from me. As soon as the elevator door closed I went toward the dude. He stood up and moved to a less populated area near the windows. We leaned against the ledge of the low windowsill and kept our voices down.

He didn't waste time on introductions. "Liu wants to talk to you. He said to tell you, you still owe us. Owe him. And one way or another he'll collect."

Figures. Jai's older brother acted like the Grand Dragon of the Triad, calling the shots. "Nothing to talk about, man. I owe him shit. I think my last message was pretty clear on that."

The messenger straightened up and glanced in the direction of the elevator where I'd sent Ivy on to Joe's room. A shiver raced down my spine at the thought he might have recognized her. Shit! Everyone at that fight would know Ivy was important to me. His gaze returned to mine and he said, "I'll be sure to tell him that. By the way nice piece of ass you got there."

"You do that." My voice went stone cold. "And tell him I don't want to see any of you anywhere near this hospital or me or mine again. The conversation won't be as pleasant as the alley. My business with the Triad is done. So is Joe's." I wanted these fuckers to know I was not some docile lamb. I wouldn't cower at their threats.

"I'll pass that on. By the way Jai's fine. You and yours will hear from him soon. And one last thing, Liu wanted me to tell you to ask Joe why your mother really died." Without another word, he stalked past me.

I stood watching him until he exited the building. The bastard had threatened me, Joe, and Ivy. I had to let Joe and Tsang know. No one would hurt Ivy. And I wondered what the hell that last crack was about my mother. She'd died in a senseless robbery. Some bastard had shot her and Joe, who'd tried to protect her. I glanced around to see if there were any more faces I recognized. Satisfied there was no danger, I pulled out my cell and called Tsang to let him know.

"I don't want you to worry about anything," Tsang said on the phone after I explained the situation. "The Tong is strong enough financially now. The Triad is hurting."

"Which makes them that much more dangerous."

"Doesn't matter, Maze. It's time to take them down. Joe

and I didn't get to these positions by accident. Tell Joe I need him out of that bed sooner rather than later and I'll be by in the morning to see him. Now you enjoy the rest of your evening with your lovely young lady. Will you go back to the condo tonight?"

"No. I'll be at Ivy's."

"All right. Just call Terry when you're ready to return. He will be with you at all times until this is over."

"One last thing, the fucker who delivered the message said I should ask Joe about why my mother died. Do you know what he meant?"

"Mind games. She died needlessly in a robbery gone bad."

"Okay, thanks. I won't raise this with Joe. You're right they're just trying to screw with us."

"I might put another familiar face in the area around you for the next couple of days too."

"Do you think…"

"Just a precaution. Now go see Joe."

Tsang disconnected the call before I could probe him further. But I already knew, the bodyguards were necessary. I shut the phone off and walked over to the elevator.

Chapter Five

Ivy

I took the elevator up to the third floor to Maze's stepfather's room. Something was definitely up, and if Maze and I stood a chance of having any kind of a future he was going to have to be honest with me. There would be no more shutting me out. No more disappearing. I wasn't stupid. I knew the sports channels didn't feature the kind of fighting he did. He told me he was done with it and I believed him, but something more was going on. We weren't being chauffeured around by his uncle's bodyguard for no reason. The elevator door opened and I followed the signs. I walked through a set of double doors and faced a nurse's station. Two nurses sat behind the counter, and one stopped me.

"Can I help you?" the blonde nurse asked.

"I'm here to see Joe Chang."

"I'll need to see some ID please," she said.

The nurse took it from me and checked her computer.

She smiled. "Room 347, honey. Last one on the left.

Follow the blue line." She raised her hand and pointed down one of four hallways branching off from around the station. I'd already been there once before so knew where to go but his room number had changed.

"Thank you," I said to her.

There were four different colors, but the blue line turned to the right and the others kept going straight. I turned right. As soon as I entered that hallway I saw the other bodyguard that had been with Mr. Tsang the night of the fight. He sat in front of one of the doors, reading a magazine. It was easy to tell these guys were bodyguards; they were all muscled and always seemed super aware of everything. I didn't have to read the room number to know it was Joe's door. I wondered if Mr. Tsang was there. The man glanced up when he saw me, and he must have recognized me.

"Good evening," he said, rising from his chair. He knocked on the door, before turning the knob and pushing it open.

"Ah, thank you," I said, moving by him and entering the room. He shut the door behind me.

Joe sat up in bed when he saw me. "Hello, there. It's good to see you again."

He looked much better than the first time I'd seen him. His skin wasn't as pale and there were no more dark circles under his eyes. A healthier glow radiated from him and his thick white hair had been combed and framed his round friendly face. The room wasn't very large and the bathroom door hung open. I walked past it toward a chair in the room. No one was in there except for Joe. Odd, what was Tsang's bodyguard doing at the door? Who was he guarding? Joe? *What the hell…*

I wanted to ask Joe what was going on, but he wasn't the person to answer my questions. I'd have to speak to Maze. So I sat down and plastered a smile on my face. "Maze will be right up. He just saw someone he knew downstairs."

Joe grinned. "Thank you for coming with him to see me. How was dinner? Maze told me you all had dinner with your mom tonight and some friends."

I smiled. Despite all of my concerns. "Dinner was great. I'm sorry my mom's not going to be in town longer to meet you, but she really liked Maze."

"I'm glad. I know he was looking forward to seeing your mom again. I'd enjoy meeting her on another visit."

I nodded. "That would be great."

"What did you think of the fight?"

"I'm not going to lie it was beautiful yet scary violent. The likes of which I've never seen and never want to see again."

He chuckled. "Yes. That's true. But Maze won't fight any more. He's agreed to just train others now."

"Yeah." I hoped it was true. "That's what he told me and I'll be glad if he does. From what I saw, he should be really good at training, too."

"He'll be the best," Joe agreed. "He'll put out champions in a year. Mark my words. In a year's time folks will line up to have a chance at training under Maze."

I smiled at his enthusiasm and thought he just might be right. For as long as I'd known him, Maze had a certain way about him. Always in total control even when things went out of control. He seemed to know what he was doing. Which made me frown again. I wasn't exactly sure why, but the information made me even more uneasy about having Tsang's bodyguards around us.

Just then Maze walked into the room. "How you feeling, Joe?" he asked as he strolled over to his stepfather, clasping his arm.

"Getting there."

Maze picked up the only other chair in the room and placed it next to me, giving me a quick kiss on the cheek before settling back into the seat.

We stayed and kept Joe company for another hour. When he shut his eyes for the third time, Maze got up. This time he kissed Joe's forehead and stepped back. "We'll come check on you tomorrow."

I rose too. "Do you know when they'll release you?" Joe had a massive heart attack, but the surgeon had done a damn good job on him. I don't know what Maze would do if he lost Joe.

"The doctor said he'd let me know tomorrow once he gets back some tests they ran today. But everything looks good so maybe in another day or so."

"That's great. We'll talk again tomorrow then, and when you're released, I'll come and get you." Maze pulled out his cell and texted Terry.

"Sounds good. Now you two leave an old man to his sleep. Go have fun."

I squeezed Joe's hand but he gripped mine and pulled me closer to him, giving me a kiss on my cheek. I beamed at him and straightened up. Maze wrapped his arm around my waist and shook Joe's hand, and then we left. The affection and love these two men had for each other ran deep. It left a warm place in my heart. I liked Joe and he seemed to have accepted me as being a part of Maze's life. I smiled thinking of Maze with my mom. I thought both of my parents would also like Joe a lot. Especially after they found out about how Joe raised Maze like a son after his mom died.

Maze told me the story one night while we just lay in bed and held each other. Yeah, Joe was a special person.

We stepped onto the elevator and I circled my arms around Maze for the short ride. I leaned against his shoulder and sighed.

"What's the matter?" he asked.

But the elevator doors opened before I could answer, and in truth, I didn't want to begin this discussion here. I just shook my head.

He placed his arm around my shoulder and we walked outside. Terry had the car sitting right at the entrance, and he stood at the door holding it open for us.

I smiled at him and got in.

"How's Joe?" he asked.

"Doing well," Maze replied. "He should be released in another day or so."

"Good to hear."

Maze got in and Terry shut the door.

Maze activated the privacy window separating us from Terry, ensuring our conversation would not be overheard. After he sat back in the seat he placed his arm around my shoulders again. "Now, tell me what's wrong?"

I shifted away from him a little. "I'm not sure. Perhaps you need to tell me."

He frowned. "Is this because I wouldn't let you wait for me earlier? Cause seriously that was nothing. I just don't want those guys anywhere near you. The less they know about you the better."

I frowned now. I had no idea what he was talking about and told him so. "What guys?" I asked. Then a light bulb went on. "Does this have something to do with that fight in the alley? I thought that guy in the waiting room seemed familiar."

He sighed and ran his free hand through his hair. "In a way. They're part of the world I've walked away from, and I don't want you anywhere near it. Okay?"

"Maze, what's going on? Are you talking about underground fighting? What you did... Was it illegal?" There'd I'd asked him. I didn't want there to be secrets between us. I loved him, and I wanted to understand him. I thought I did, he was trying to protect me. But I needed him to know he could trust me. I'd never betray him. But I also didn't want him having anything to do with that side of his life ever again either. I watched him cripple a man the other night. No, this was no world for me, but Maze didn't belong here either. No matter how much he seemed to fit in. Maze fought when cornered.

He put his hand on the side of my face and I leaned into

the caress. "I don't deserve you. I know that. But I swear, as long as there's breath in my body, I will spend every day loving you. Making you happy." He moved his hand to grasp mine like he needed the contact.

Threading our fingers together, he spoke again. "As much as I didn't want you to, you saw for yourself what I do is dangerous. And yes, it straddles the line. Hell, most of the time it falls right into the other side. But I've always fought a clean fight. I've never thrown one. The people who run these competitions wanted me to throw the fight the other night."

"Oh my God!" I gripped his hand tighter. In fact, I placed my other hand over our joined hands. "But you won. So you didn't go through with it. You did the right thing."

Even in the dimness of the car I still saw his slight smile. "Yeah, I did. I didn't hold back."

A thought occurred to me. "Wait. Is that why they changed fighters for the second part? After the first guy got hurt I didn't understand why the fight wasn't called then."

He nodded. "Normally it would have been but it wasn't a normal fight. So they put in a replacement."

"Yeah, one who had your uncle furious? I looked at Mr. Tsang's face when they made the announcement."

"Yes. Even though there aren't many rules in the arena, that particular fighter who challenged me pays attention to none of them. He's been banned from most of the underground groups, because of the way he fights. To kill or maim. But when I faced him I couldn't focus on any of that because I wasn't going to lose. Not with you sitting in the audience."

"Don't say that."

"Why? It's true."

I hugged him to me. "I don't care. I never want you to fight again."

"I'm not. I told you that was my last fight. Uncle Tsang and Joe have seen to that."

"So what happens now? Since you didn't throw the fight. Is that why we have the bodyguards? Are you in trouble?"

He shook his head. "That's just Uncle Tsang being extra careful. They're there as more of a statement. Uncle Tsang is part of the group that regulates these fights. It's his way of letting them know that he supports me, and my decision to fight clean. Besides, the fact my gym will be open to all will ensure they leave me alone."

Now it was my turn to shake my head. "Wow. This is just not a world I really understand."

He kissed my forehead. "No worries, babe. You shouldn't, and you won't have to. It's all good now."

On the one hand, I understood Maze withheld information from me in order to protect me. But on the other hand... "I'm not a child, Maze. I get it, okay? And I understand that you can't go into details with me about what you were involved in. Or even your uncle's involvement. I get that he might operate in a way requiring bodyguards. But I want us to be a normal couple with a normal life. Well, as normal as a dancer who might not dance again and an ex-MMA fighter can be."

I reached up to him and placed both hands on the sides of his perfectly chiseled face. "That means no more secrets. I believe you when you say you're out. But we need to be honest with each other. Otherwise what we have isn't real. We can't rely on each other if we don't have faith in one another." At my words his body tensed against mine. "Are you in danger because you didn't do what these people wanted? And don't you dare repeat what you just said. Tell me the truth."

Chapter Six

Maze

God I loved her. I raised my hands and placed them over hers. Twining our fingers together, I placed our joined hands in her lap. How did I answer her so she didn't run away from me? I couldn't lose her. Without her beside me, I would only be taking up space. She gave my life meaning. But at the same time I still had to protect her. Even if it was from myself.

I took a deep breath. "I'm not sure. And that's the truth. It's also true that Uncle Tsang is trying to handle this in a way that I'll be left alone. I don't know the details nor do I want to know. Nor do you."

She leaned forward and kissed me then pulled back. "Thank you. And no more running away and trying to shelter me. Whatever is going on just let me know. We are in this together, okay? That's what loving someone is about. Going through the good and the bad. When…when Shelly died you tried to be there for me and I withdrew. Closed in on myself."

I froze. The fact she brought up Shel after all these years like this was huge for us. I always felt one reason she pulled away from me was because she blamed me somewhat for what happened. And I stayed away from her because I knew the harshness of the life I was getting involved in. I didn't try hard enough to reach across the miles separating us and hold us together.

"I should have done more to draw you out," I offered.

She smiled sadly. "Maybe. But even if you did I'm not sure you'd have been able to do it from Japan. We both needed to go our own way back then. It was the right thing to do. We had to grow separately I think to fully understand what it means to be together. I...I never let you know how much your text on the day...Shel died meant to me. No one, not even my folks or hers, ever thought to check up on me on that date. You were the only one who seemed to understand. It held me together. For a long time I blamed myself, you. If I hadn't been with you I would have been, should have been with her."

Her eyes filled with tears and I wiped them away with my thumb. "Shhh, it was not your fault. My God, you could have been in the golf cart that night with her and she would probably still have been driving."

"That's all true. I hated driving and Shel loved the carts. We'd taken that same dangerous path many nights during the summer at the beach. And I know she would have been drunk. I had been drinking that night, too. I no longer blame myself, or you. I haven't for a long time now, but your texts meant a lot to me. It kept me close to Shel on a day when I needed someone to acknowledge she once lived. What she meant to me. You did. So thank you for that."

I wrapped my arms around her and drew her to me, but before I could do anything else the car pulled up in front of her condo.

"We're here," Terry said needlessly through the speaker.

I glanced up. Yep, we were. I untangled us and by the time I reached for the door handle it was already being opened for me.

We went up to her place and after Ivy opened the door we found the condo dark. I remembered she'd left a lamp on near the windows when we'd left earlier. But Dante could have turned them off. No sooner did I think that when I realized there was someone on the couch. In fact, two someones. One on top of the other and they were as still as stone. From the whiff of sex in the air I knew what they were doing.

I put my arm around Ivy and guided her to her room

without looking in the direction of the couch or who was on it. It wasn't until we got to her room and closed the door that she sat on her bed and giggled.

"Oh, God. I'm glad it was dark in there." She laughed. "I wonder who Dante's hooking up with now?"

"Don't know and don't care." And I didn't as long as it wasn't Ivy. He and I had made peace but I wasn't stupid. I knew if I blew it he'd be right there to console her. Fucker. And that is exactly what he'd been doing.

"I wonder if it's a guy? Oh my God, I so do not need to see that, or him with Christy either." She began to laugh again and put her hand over her mouth to stifle her mirth.

I smiled, she's so naïve. Then I frowned. Maybe it was getting too crowded with us all here. We'd been spending most of the time at Ivy's only going back to my place in Brooklyn a couple of times over the last few days. Mostly because the condo was near the hospital. But Joe hopefully would be out in another day or so, and I needed to turn my attention to the gym. There was a nice two-bedroom apartment on the second floor of the building. I knew I owned the building, but if the apartment was rented out I didn't know if I'd be able to break someone's lease. I remembered Uncle Tsang told Joe how he'd had it renovated a year ago and rented it out. It was why, when we'd made plans to return to the U.S., we didn't stay there. I wondered if may be it was now available? I'd check first thing in the morning. Once Ivy's cast came off it would be easy for me to help her exercise every day so she could dance again. If the apartment was available it might be a good place for us, Ivy and me. That is, if she even wanted to be with me 24/7.

I watched her beautiful smile, she was probably still thinking about walking in on Dante and his friend. But my thoughts held my attention. I couldn't believe I actually stood there, leaning against the door, contemplating setting up house with someone. Living with someone. In truth, the idea of getting that close to anyone, willingly making such a commitment, had never entered my consciousness. Anyone that was, except for Ivy. Yes. I want to be with this girl 24/7. The idea should have freaked me out. Instead, my heart filled with joy at the thought of sleeping and waking with her in my arms. Every fucking night. Damn, my dick twitched.

The way she made me feel so good, went beyond the rocket to mars sex we shared. I wanted us to build a life and grow together. Hell, someday maybe even have kids together. Shit. Where did that come from? But I knew in my gut. I loved her. That's all there was to it.

"Why are you standing way over there?" she asked once she stopped giggling.

"I've just been thinking about something."

She sat up as if she sensed my seriousness.

"How would you feel about the two of us getting a place together?"

She stared right back at me her eyes wide. I could tell I surprised her with my question. "I don't know. I guess I never really thought about it. What about Dante?"

I shook my head. "He's already got this condo, and you told me he could afford this place on his own. I'm thinking maybe he needs his own space, as do you and I. I love you, Ivy. I want to be with you all the time." I pushed myself away from the door and walked over to the bed and then sat beside her. Taking one of her hands in mine I raised it to my lips and brushed a kiss over her knuckles.

"I like falling asleep with me curled around you and waking up with you curled around me. I like us planning out our days the night before or that morning. I like that you know where I am and that I'm coming home to you. I like it all and I want it all with you."

Damn, I was no poet, but I needed her to know how I felt. I wanted all of those things but I also wanted to protect her. Just in case. I could do it in the part of Chinatown Tsang controlled, and better at the gym. It was neutral ground, but also the Tong owned most of the businesses on that street. I knew who the ruling Triad members were in the area, but I figure I needed to get to know the legit business owners that made up the Tong now, too. By taking over the gym and retiring from fighting, I'd become one of them. I was probably their youngest member. Chinatown wasn't as large an area as it used to be and it was mostly evenly matched up now between Triad and Tong, as to who owned what.

I looked into the eyes of the woman I loved for such a very long time and waited for her to tell me we'd build a life together. Yeah, I wanted us to live together, but I wanted more for us, too. First, I needed to show her I'd be able to take care of her in all ways.

She clutched my hand. "Are you sure, Maze? That's a big step."

"I'm ready. And someday I will offer you even more."

Her eyes went even wider at my words. The brown in her pupils seemed to glow before her next words put a punch in my gut. "I love you so much. Don't let me down."

"I promise I won't."

"All right."

I leaned into her and captured her mouth again. When I could bring myself to separate I told her, "Tomorrow morning I'm already scheduled to meet with Uncle Tsang and a contractor but I'm going to call him first and I want you to come with me. There's an apartment over the gym. I'm not sure if it's available but if it is we can take a look at it. See if you like it and if you want anything changed. If it's not or you don't like it then we can look for something else nearby."

"Sounds like a plan."

I folded her in my arms and together we lay back on the bed and just held on to each other, content to merely be, for now.

****

The next morning, Terry dropped us off at the gym. I pushed against the entrance door and it opened. The gym was closed but we were expected. As soon as we walked into the place we found Uncle Tsang near the main training ring waiting for us. He wasn't alone. There were two other men with him. The tall portly guy with a tool belt strapped around his girth I figured for the contractor, and the tall thin one with the briefcase, the equipment rep. I'd spoken to Tsang earlier this morning and he said the apartment was vacant. The tenant had cleared out last week. So the apartment was mine to do what I wanted.

First, we went through the main floor that made up the gym. There were two locker rooms. Men and women. A massage room, two offices, and two private training rooms.

These were on the perimeter of the main training area, which held exercise equipment, and, of course, the fighting ring sat dead center of it all. Not a whole lot needed to be done to the place. We'd just have to bring in some new equipment and replace a few things. Ivy suggested redoing the shower areas. They were pretty beat up, and she had some great ideas.

We took the private elevator near the office in the gym to look at the apartment. Which could also be accessed directly from the street entrance by a set of stairs. The layout was pretty sweet. To my surprise I found three bedrooms and not the two I originally thought. One was considerably smaller and could be used as an office. The walls were all brick. The floor looked like some sort of stained burnt bronze cement. Two of the bedrooms had smoky sliding glass doors and the third a traditional door. The place held lots of windows and open space. But all that mattered was Ivy loved it. Only one problem—no furniture. So an hour after leaving the gym, that's what we were doing. Who would have thought me, Mr. Tough Guy, would be fucking furniture shopping? I didn't care how I looked. I would have dragged a fucking couch through Chinatown if that's what my Ivy wanted.

"So when are you going to tell Dante?" I asked, as I held the door open for Ivy at the ABC Carpet & Home store.

We'd just spent the last three hours there. Next time someone says the words shopping and furniture together I might have to drop 'em. This shit was exhausting. We explored eight floors of any and everything you might need, or not, for your home.

"When we get back to the condo." She shrugged.

I was glad she didn't appear to have a problem breaking it to Dante that he was losing his roomy. "Good, cause the mattress will be delivered tomorrow and I want us in our own apartment by tomorrow night." It was true. I'd arranged to have the furniture delivered within the next week. The bed frame wouldn't get there until after the mattress. A few things would take longer. But for the first time in my life I was creating a home, for Ivy. I should be scared as shit because I didn't know what the hell I was doing. But damned if I wasn't excited to keep house with her.

"When are you going to tell Joe?" she countered.

"He already knows. Tsang told him when I asked him about the apartment this morning. They were going to offer it to me. Joe will stay with Tsang for a few days after he gets out of the hospital. So I'd like to stop by my place first and pack up some stuff and then we can go to the condo and get some of yours."

"Okay but it's going to take more than one trip. I'll

probably need a couple of days."

"That's fine. I travel light, not much to move. I've got about two suitcases to fill, a couple boxes, and I'll be done." Soon as I spoke, my phone chimed that I had a text. I checked it. "Feel like going to a party tonight?" I asked Ivy.

"Party? Whose?"

"Vin. A good friend of mine. He and I fought once in Japan when I first got there and we keep in touch." By nature fighters were competitors so it was difficult to make friends with someone you might have to kick the shit out of. But Vin was different. "He's pretty cool. He returned to the U.S. a couple of years ago and stops by the gym to keep in shape. He no longer fights but he follows the fighting circuit. And if I know him he bet on my fight."

"Did he bet on you?"

I grinned. "Damn straight."

"I'd love to meet your friend. Do you want to go?"

I nodded. "It might be fun."

"Okay then."

Grinning, I texted Vin back.

Chapter Seven

Ivy

I wasn't exactly sure what to expect at this party, given a former fighter hosted it. I was shocked when Terry dropped us off at the 230 Fifth bar. The roof top club on Fifth Avenue was really nice. His friend had rented out the place for the night.

"What does this Vin do now?" I asked.

"Some kind of stock broker."

I glanced at Maze. "I thought the market was bad?"

Maze looked around at the opulence and crowd. "Apparently not for everyone."

"Maze! Man!"

I turned around at the voice booming over the music, only to stare at the dark shirt-covered chest of the person calling Maze's name. I leaned against my crutch as my eyes traveled upward. I had to tilt my head back to see his face. Holy Shit! This dude was huge. He made linemen look short and skinny. And Maze fought him and beat him.

My gaze returned to Maze who grinned back at the guy and had already taken a sideways step toward him in greeting. He had his arm raised, bent at the elbow, and held in front while he leaned in close and sorta kinda hugged the other person. I hid a smile. Such a guy.

"Vin. Hey, man. How's it hanging?" Maze said.

Vin smiled and his gaze shifted to me. Maze still held my hand and I knew it wasn't lost on Vin. "Pretty damn fine from where I'm standing," Vin said.

"And if you want to stay standing don't touch." Maze smirked, then introduced us. "Ivy this is our host, Vin. Vin, my girl, Ivy."

Vin's eyebrows rose to almost touch his hairline. "No, shit. It's nice to meet you, Ivy. So this is the one?"

"The only," Maze beamed.

I glanced back and forth between them missing something. "What?"

"I saw a poster of you once in his room," Vin volunteered.

"What?" I repeated confused. I'd been to Maze's room. There was no poster of me. But when I looked at Maze, damned even in the dull lighting I could see his blush.

"Ah, yeah. I had posters of some of your performances in my place back in Japan."

I was intrigued. "Oh. Where are they now?"

Maze rubbed the back of his neck. "Ah, still in my room here. I just put them in the closet."

I grinned. He was so cute when he blushed, and Vin cracked up, patting him on the back.

Vin glanced at my crutch then down at my cast enclosed foot. "What happened to you?"

I could get around on only one crutch now. "I pulled a tendon."

He winced. "Ouch."

"She'll be fine." Maze held me tighter against his side. I loved his optimism.

Vin placed his hand on Maze's shoulder. "Hey, man, that was one wicked ass fight. I've never seen you move better. And I just want to thank you for the money I made off that fight." He waved his other hand around. "It helped pay for this little party here," Vin laughed.

Someone called his name and he turned in that direction then nodded. "I gotta make my rounds but I'll come back. Have fun." He shook Maze's hand. "Ivy, real nice meeting you."

"You, too," I replied.

Vin gave me a quick hug then got swallowed up amongst the bodies.

"Come on," Maze said, moving farther toward the center of the roof.

Good thing the place wasn't too packed. Not like the only other time I'd been there. If it were I'd have had a hard time maneuvering through a crowd on a crutch.

It was a little chilly up there, but the heaters placed throughout took the edge off. The view of the Empire State Building and the skyline of the city was stunning and worth a little shiver. We found a low sofa for two and Maze took my crutch and placed it against the arm. Before we sat down, he pushed the table away a little more so I could stretch my leg out. His thoughtfulness warmed me to my soul.

"This is a great view," he said, twisting to look at the vista over his shoulder then he looked back at me. I shivered.

Maze wrapped his arm around me. "Cold?"

"No, a little warm actually." And I was. My reaction had nothing to do with the external temperature but the way he made me feel. Excited.

Maze found us a spot right near a heater and I took off my jacket. A waitress came over to us and asked if we needed anything from the bar. She also left us a little platter of appetizers.

"Nice," I said when she walked away. "Your friend certainly knows how to throw a party.

Maze chuckled. "Yeah, he does." He picked up a little puff creation off the plate and held it in front of my mouth. "Open."

He placed it on my tongue but I clamped my lips around his finger so he had to pull it out. He did, real slow. "Damn girl."

I grinned, chewed, and then leaned forward to kiss him. The waitress came back with our drinks and she placed a large red reserved sign on the table in front of our seats. "If you wish to move around this should ensure your place is saved."

"Thanks," Maze said.

After she moved off, he picked up his shot of Cuervo Gold and I grabbed my beer. "To us." He raised his glass toward me and I clinked my bottle against it.

"To us," he repeated.

We drank and I swayed in my seat to the rhythm of the music. It had been too long since I danced. And I hated it.

"Do you want to dance?" Maze asked.

"I want to, just not sure with this stupid cast."

"Come on." He insisted as he grabbed the crutch near him and handed it to me. He stood up and moved aside, pushing the table out so it was easier for me to hobble past it. Then he led us to the dance floor. We stayed toward the edge of it and danced. I'd never enjoyed dancing more. Maze took my crutch, but placed my arms around his neck. Hanging onto my crutch, he wrapped his arms around my waist, holding me up and we gently moved from side to side.

After we danced a few songs he asked, "Ready to sit down?"

"Yeah, I'm getting a little tired."

He led the way back to our table, but as I glanced past him I saw a couple of guys sitting there, and a third standing behind the seat. I'd left my jacket draped over the back of it yet people still sat there, ignoring the red reserved sign. Where was our waitress?

I rested my hand on Maze's shoulder, and I felt the muscles in his shoulder tense. Despite that, he didn't stop walking until we reached the table.

"I believe those seats are reserved for us," he stated. His voice low and cold. I'd never heard him speak that way. Not even the last couple of times I'd been with him when he fought. I prayed this wasn't going to revert into one of those. I couldn't take it.

Please no.

"Maze, right?"

What? The guy knew him?

The one who'd spoken had Asian features but his hair

was dyed white blond and he had black roots. The other person seated next to him also had Asian features but his hair was black. Both men appeared slender and perhaps Maze's height.

Maze didn't reply, but the freeze radiating off his body, if such a thing were possible, sent a chill down my spine. I kept a grip on Maze's shoulder, trying to hold him back but knowing if he decided to fight I would not be able to stop him.

His silence didn't prevent the man from continuing to talk like Maze had replied. "Yeah. Saw you fight the other night. I lost a shit load of money. But you already knew that."

Still Maze said nothing.

The guy smirked. Clearly, he planned to bait Maze. "Since you are Maze and I don't see that name here, as far as I'm concerned this table was reserved for me."

"I don't see your name on it either," Maze countered.

"Yes, you do. It's reserved," Maze's tormentor said. The other guy sitting beside him and the one hovering in the back of the couch laughed their asses off. Just then the waitress showed up.

"Excuse me," she said. "That seat's already taken."

"Yeah, by me," Asshole answered, snickering.

"It's okay," Maze said, "We're checking out."

I slipped my hand off Maze's shoulder and entwined our fingers. He squeezed them.

"Oh...okay," the waitress replied. "There's no charge, Vin took care of it. Excuse me," she said. She leaned near asshole to grab the jacket I'd left on the sofa. She had to tug it because the dude leaned back against it and didn't seem to want to budge. Maze squeezed my hand even harder, but the waitress managed to yank the jacket and handed it to Maze.

"Thanks," he said and he turned around. I didn't have to be told twice to get the hell outta there. I almost stumbled when I heard the last taunt.

"Pity you turned out to be such a pussy and quit the arena before I could cut your ass down."

I didn't dare slacken my hold on Maze's hand. I kept moving and he remained walking alongside me. We took the elevator to the exit level. Maze pulled his phone out and texted Terry. We made it out of the club and the car was there to greet us. I wasn't sure Terry even moved from the spot. It wasn't until Maze and I sat safely in the car that I was able to exhale. I turned and stared at Maze. His gaze remained straight ahead, his profile rigid with anger. That was okay. I was fine with that, and it was understandable. But I was proud he hadn't given into it. He'd told me the truth; he wasn't fighting any more. I leaned against him and he turned his head looking right at me.

He sighed. "I'm sorry about that. Sorry our night out got ruined."

Raising his arm, he placed it over my shoulder and pulled me closer to him. I lifted my leg and placed it over his. He leaned into me in response, kissing my neck.

The rigidness of his body relaxed more as he leaned against mine. I put my palm on his face, and his warmth rushed into me. "No. There's nothing for you to be sorry about. I had a great evening with you. Love you."

"Love you, too." He shifted and pulled out his phone. "I'm just texting Vin to let him know we bounced and I'll catch him later."

"I liked him."

"Yeah, he's one of the good ones."

"Did you…did you know those other guys?"

He raked his fingers through his soft silky hair. "Only the one doing the talking and only by reputation."

"Is he a fighter?"

"Yes. But I never fought him. And won't now."

I smiled at the grim expression on his face. "I'm glad you didn't let them get to you."

"It wasn't easy, but it's time for me to learn to walk

away." He combed his fingers through my wavy curls. The man had a hair fetish. "I have you to thank for that. I know you don't like me fighting and I promised you I won't outside of training."

"Yes, you did, and I see you're a man of your word."

"I promised you something else, too. Someday I want to give you everything. Don't give up on me, okay?"

I smiled and nodded. I glanced out the window to see where we were and realized Terry was taking us back to Chinatown. "Are we headed to Chinatown tonight?"

"Yes." He nuzzled my neck. "I got text confirmation earlier and forgot to tell you. The mattress got delivered this evening. I had one of the managers at the gym let them in. So we have a mattress to break in."

"I do like the way you think."

My phone rang. It was a call from my mom. I glanced at Maze and mouthed, "My mom." He kissed the side of my neck as I accepted the call and sat quietly next to me rubbing my thigh. Mom just wanted me to know she'd arrived home safely. They all did.

I hung up and smiled at Maze. "Mom said to tell you hi and that she enjoyed meeting you again."

"Me, too. I noticed you didn't mention your new living arrangements."

I sighed. So much was going on with my folks and their best friends right now. I didn't want to discuss my new living arrangements on the phone. "The surgery is confirmed, so I'll be there next week. I'm thinking it's best to tell her in person."

He nodded. "I can be there on the day of surgery. Do you want to wait until I get there?"

"No. I need to talk to them first on my own. Besides, I want to tell them as soon as I see them. It will be at least another day or so before you can get there right?"

In truth, I wanted to tell my mom right away. Not sure about my dad. And it was probably best I tell him alone anyway. Even though Maze wanted to do this with me. But I needed to let my mom, at least know sooner rather than later. Maze couldn't be with me the entire visit. He needed to be in town next week for some of the deliveries, and to make sure the work got done so the gym could reopen under new ownership in a couple of weeks. Not that his being there would help or hurt when I told my parents we'd moved in together. I knew mom would be okay but dad. Not so sure.

"Yeah," he said. "But if you need me to be there when you tell them then I'll reschedule the deliveries and be there."

I smiled. "Thanks, but it's fine."

"You're sure?"

"Yes." And I was surer than anything in my life. No matter what, I belonged with Maze.

The limo pulled up to our building. Maze helped me out of the car. For the first time we used the street entrance. When Maze opened the door of our new home, he scooped me up in his arms. "Put your arm around my neck."

"Maze, what are you doing?"

"Carrying you across the threshold of our new home."

I grinned. "That's for brides."

"One day you will be. Mine that is."

The motion of my heart paused between beats. That's what he did to me. "Maze..."

He lowered his mouth and kissed me. At the same time I heard the door slam shut, I assumed he kicked it closed. Turning around he had me flip the dead bolt to lock the downstairs entrance. I held onto my crutch and Maze, while he held onto me. He walked us up several flights of stairs. Once we got to the landing, he went down a short hallway to stop at our door. He shifted me so he could get the keys out of his pocket and unlocked the apartment. He carried me across the threshold, then kicked this door shut, too.

"Lock this one also, will ya, babe?" he directed me.

I reached down and did as he asked. Not once did he put

me down. Not that there was any place to put me. The apartment was practically empty. He headed straight for the master bedroom. The mattress sat on the floor. Beside it were three suitcases Terry had dropped off for us earlier. Two of them belonged to Maze.

He placed me gently on the mattress, then took the crutch away from me and rested it on the floor. Returning to me, he removed my jacket and shirt, kissing my skin every time he saw it exposed. He moved to kiss my belly button before reaching down with his hand to remove my black stretch yoga pants. They were the only kind of pants I could wear with my cast. He carefully got them off my legs, leaving me only in my gray lacy underwear, which he himself had placed on me earlier that morning. He seemed to love dressing and undressing me. I was totally fine with that.

I enjoyed watching the way his muscles rippled as he raised his arm to remove his own clothing. He took off everything a little too fast for me, but the view of a stripped down Maze was delectable and nothing to complain about.

He placed one knee on the mattress, and his dick twitched, brushing against the side of my thigh. It appeared eager to touch me, as eager as I was for its touch. I smiled as he pulled the last barrier between us off, my panty.

Chapter Eight

Maze

"You are so beautiful." And she was, every luscious curve, her kind heart, every part of her. All mine. I don't know what I ever did in my life to be granted someone like her. I knew I'd fucked up in the past and I'd try not to again because I couldn't lose her. I'd do whatever I had to, to deserve her love.

She moved her arm and wrapped it around my neck, drawing me to her. I covered her body with mine. I intended to go slow but wasn't sure either of us wanted slow right now. This was our first night in our place. I smiled. Plenty of time to do slow later.

She opened her legs and I kissed her at the same time I lowered my hand to cup her. I ended up moaning into her mouth. She was so fucking wet and ready for me. My dick didn't have to be told twice.

I grasped the pulsating length and guided it straight to where it throbbed to go, to where it needed to go. As soon as

I entered her she sighed, a sound of pure pleasure humming from her throat, and she grabbed my ass. She flexed her hips upward and I pushed inward, diving deeper into my haven. I pulled out just to her entrance and she shifted one leg farther up on me. I moved my arms under her knees and raised them until they were over my shoulder, leaving her very open and vulnerable to me.

I surged all the way inside her, then out again, and then in again. Soon we had our rhythm, and she met me thrust for thrust. When she reached between our bodies and grasped my balls, my entire body clenched. I roared while I released everything into her. My frame kept shuddering until all the liquid seemed to be drained from my cock. And still I wanted to give up more. I didn't care how many times I'd made love with Ivy, I always wanted more. Finally, my trembling stopped and the quivers coming from her sex slowed to the point I could breathe again. Barely.

I lowered her legs then rolled to the side. My dick had softened and slipped out of her. My breathing evened out more as we lay side by side staring at each other. I pushed the hair off her face and leaned forward to kiss the tip of her button nose.

"Love you," I whispered and settled my head on the pillow next to hers. More content than I've ever been in my life.

"I love you, too."

An annoying sound kept playing in my head, trying to drag me out of the cocoon of peace surrounding me. I attempted to ignore it, but Ivy moving out of my arms had me opening my eyes and awareness coming that made me realize the noise came from my ringing cell.

I sat up and glanced around. Floor. The phone was in my pants pocket on the floor.

I rolled over Ivy and reached down to answer the call but it stopped ringing as soon as I touched it. It was a missed call from Uncle Tsang, and my fuzzy brain also registered the time. A few minutes after three a.m. Nothing good could come from a phone call at this witching hour, something Joe used to say about late night calls. I sat up, but before I could hit redial, the phone vibrated again. My hand was fucking trembling when I hit the answer button to take the call my gut screamed would change everything.

I held the phone up to my ear and listened. Blood exploded in my head and the phone fell from my icy fingers to the mattress. I couldn't think. I watched as Ivy picked up the phone and spoke quickly to Uncle Tsang. When she hung up there were tears in her eyes.

"Yes. We have to go." I didn't recognize the dead voice coming from my mouth. I still hadn't completely processed what I'd heard. Somehow she got me out of bed. I don't know what I would have done without Ivy. I'm not sure how I even managed to get dressed and downstairs to the car. Terry was already there in the driver's seat, and there was another large guy waiting for us on the sidewalk, long black hair pulled back into a braid and built like a soma wrestler.

"This way, sir," he said gesturing toward the open car door as he kept glancing up and down the street. He helped us into the limo then got into the passenger seat.

It wasn't until I stuck my head in the car I realized that wasn't Terry behind the wheel but Will. The other bodyguard I'd seen a few times at Tsang's side, he had Asian features but seemed to be more of a mix. But he had the same muscular built as the others but kept his hair short cropped.

His presence brought me a little out of my stupor. "What's going on, Will?" I asked as I sat down. "Where's Terry?"

"I'll have you there in five, Maze. Hang on," Will said. "Mr. Tsang will fill you in. This is Mark and he'll be with you for awhile, too." Mark sat in the front seat and glanced over his shoulder and nodded.

I put my head back, shut my eyes and shut down my thought processes. Ivy spoke, I think she said thank you to Will. My mind returned to its daze. One word kept ricocheting around in my head—shot. Joe had been shot and Terry wasn't driving us.

The pressure of Ivy's hand in mine caused me to open my eyes and turn at the same time to stare at her. The fear and worry I saw in her eyes reflected in my own emotions, but I couldn't reassure her or comfort her. And she couldn't comfort me. We'd both been here before almost five years ago. I knew she hurt back then and I didn't know how to take the pain away. There were no words we needed to share now. We only needed each other.

When she leaned forward I took her mouth and devoured her. My fingers dug into her arms, and my chest rose and fell to the point of pain. She became the only thing keeping the darkness threatening to engulf me in check. She must have known what I needed and didn't deny me. Instead, she placed her palms on my face and kissed me back just as hard as I kissed her. I relaxed my manic hold on her, pulled back and took a deep breath. After a moment, I placed my head against hers.

The car came to a screeching halt and the door opened. I stepped out and turned back to help Ivy out of the car. I didn't realize Mark had hopped out of the car and stood by the open door. I didn't know him but I figured since he was with Will and Tsang sent him it meant he could be trusted.

He kept glancing around, scanning the area. He nodded at Will then he turned back to us. "Stay with me. We're going straight in. I know where your uncle is waiting for us."

I was glad cause I wasn't sure I'd be too coherent right now. My world was crumbling and I held onto the only thing that mattered in it any more, Ivy.

He led us straight to the elevators and we got in. I have no clue what floor we got off on but when the elevator door opened a man slightly shorter than I, with his familiar bald head and round face stood there to meet us. I stepped off and Uncle Tsang hugged me then Ivy.

"How is he?" Ivy asked. I'm glad she did. I couldn't.

He didn't say anything. Just took my arm, and I gripped Ivy's hand like a lifeline as I followed Uncle Tsang to some room that looked like a waiting area but it was small. It had two long couches, a few chairs, and a television set on the wall that was turned off. Someone closed the door behind us, another one of Tsang's guards. Mark remained outside with him.

"Sit down, Maze," Uncle Tsang said.

I shook my head. "No. Tell me."

Tsang's gaze shifted to Ivy, a helpless look in his eyes before he focused on me again. It was then I knew. I saw it when he looked at me.

My legs. Suddenly, I couldn't feel them. Tsang caught me and helped me to a chair. I stared up at him, tears already fighting for space in my eyes. "What…is he…" I couldn't finish the thought.

"I'm sorry, Maze." There were tears in Uncle Tsang's eyes. He did nothing to hide them or stop them when they spilled down his cheeks.

"No." I thought the word came out as a scream. That's what it felt like in my head but it sounded more like a croak, born of pain. "No," I said, stronger this time.

"He died before he got here. They worked on him the entire time in the ambulance and more when we first arrived but he never regained consciousness. He's gone Maze. Joe's gone."

Sobs racked my body. My head dropped to my chest. I felt Ivy fall to my feet rather than saw her, but even through the pain, I knew she was there. I needed her so badly. Her hands tightened around my own and I gripped them. They were the only things keeping me from punching a wall.

"Maze," she wailed. "I'm so sorry." She looked up. "Mr. Tsang, what happened?"

My head snapped up, tears still coursing down my face. "What the fuck happened? What do you mean before he got here? Where was he? You were supposed to protect him. How the fuck did he get shot?"

My breath hitched when I noticed the blood. All on the arm of Tsang's jacket and I knew whose it was. I had to take a deep breath and almost choked on it. "Fuck. Fuck."

He gripped my shoulder. "You have every right to be angry. Let me explain. We made a mistake. I made a mistake. They…we were ambushed. I'd arranged for Joe to be moved from the hospital earlier this morning. I thought by doing it at an odd hour, there'd be less chance of any problems. But they must have been watching, waiting."

He paused and took a deep breath. "Along the way a trash truck blocked the road on a one way street and our car had to stop. I heard shots, they took out the tires. We decided to get out of the car because we were vulnerable. The windows are bullet proof but the entire body of the car isn't. Only the doors. So we tried to make a run for it. But they picked their location well. They had a shooter on one of the buildings and men behind the trash truck. Terry and Jason, my other guard, were with us. We all managed to make it out of the car and huddled behind the open rear door using it as cover. We stayed low, kept the car between the sharpshooter and us. We were going to make our way to the parked cars to give ourselves better cover. But the sharpshooter fired off more shots pinning us there just as more men came from around the truck. Jason and I managed to shoot two of them, but while three came from the front one came up from the rear. He fired twice, first hitting Terry and Joe stepped out..."

Tsang lost it. I'd never seen him cry. The man broke down and cried. Ivy released one of my hands to hug his bicep with her arm. He took a handkerchief out of his pocket and wiped at his face, then he continued. "Joe pushed me. The son of a bitch pushed me to the ground. The second shot hit his head. The shooter got away."

Leaning forward I wrapped my arms around Ivy and bawled like a baby into her hair. At some point I stopped and the doctor came into the room. He explained the medical terms as to what happened but who gave a shit?

"Doctor, is he dead?" I asked, needing the confirmation. I had to hear it myself to accept it. I had to.

"Yes, Mr. Chang, I'm sorry. There wasn't anything we could do."

"Thank you." Cause dead was dead. I really didn't need to hear more about complications and hemorrhaging. I already knew the goddamn cause. "I need to see him,

Doctor."

After that they took us to the room where Joe still laid, a sheet over his face. I held onto Ivy.

I let go of her before reaching out to lift the sheet off his face. I had to see for myself. To know for sure, it was my father in so many ways who lay there. Even by blood since he'd shed it for me. One of the earliest memories I have of Joe was of him crawling into the back room to get me that day…that day my mother died. He looked like he was in pain then. There was blood on his face and he had fear in his eyes. Even as a child I knew that. Looking at him now, while his eyes were closed his features took me back to that day. To the memory I'd just been able to recall. A day of so much pain. He took me out of the store so I never saw my mother's body on the floor in the front room. I had enough nightmares as a child as it was, I didn't need any more. Now I had one more to add to the night demons. I leaned down and kissed Joe's cheek, before lowering the cover back over his face.

"Let me see you home, Maze." Tsang sighed. "I'll make arrangements for Joe. Will and Mark will take you back to my condo in Chinatown. You'll be safer there. I will sort this out. I promise you. I swear on my friendship with Joe."

I turned to look at the man that truly had been like an uncle to me. "Thank you, Uncle Tsang. But after you're done here. I have questions."

I glanced at Ivy who had been softly crying beside me, her arm plastered around my waist. I encircled her in my embrace and placed my lips at her temple.

"Come on," I said to her.

Mark waited for us on the other side of the door and he took us out of the hospital. I saw the familiar black limo with Will behind the wheel. We got in and Will drove off. It hit me then as I watched him drive us in a world that had suddenly become so dark.

Terry was gone, too. The numbness that had begun to invade my limbs since I got the phone call enveloped me completely. I wondered if I'd ever feel again.

Twenty minutes later, I sat on the long comfortable couch at Tsang's place with Ivy spread out beside me. His entire condo was homey done in a combo Marta Steward meets the Ming Dynasty style with its peacock blue, green and dark brown accents.

I was glad we were there. Ivy's legs rested on the couch and her head in my lap. She slept while I played with her hair, touching it lightly, her face, her arm. But I couldn't sleep. My mind raced with thoughts I shouldn't have while I held Ivy in my arms. Our connection was the only thing barely grounding me, because the deadness inside still hadn't gone away.

A soft knock preceded the door opening, and Uncle Tsang entered the condo. I put my finger up to my lips so he wouldn't say anything to wake up Ivy.

Gently, I eased myself up and placed a cushion under her head. I bent down and kissed her brow and then motioned to Uncle Tsang to follow me to his den. As soon as we entered the room, I closed the door. He headed for the liquor cabinet and took out two glasses. He poured dark-colored elixirs into both. But no amount of the stuff in my veins could fix this. He offered one glass to me before sitting in the chair in front of the desk. I took a good swallow. I didn't sit down.

He reached into his inside jacket pocket. "Here," he said, handing me an envelope.

I frowned. "What's this?" But as I glanced down at it, it had my name scrawled across the front and I recognized the handwriting. "Joe?" I looked at Tsang and he nodded.

"Open it."

My hands shook as I tore open the envelope.

Dear Maze,

I gave this to Uncle Tsang to give to you just in case I couldn't be there to tell you myself. The doctors are optimistic about my health. So far so good, but in this world nothing is guaranteed, and I needed you to know about the past from me. Tsang told me what that Triad messenger said to you and I thought you deserved the whole truth. It's time.

You know only part of my history with the Triad. You know I was a member because of my controlling interest in the Tong. What you do not know is that I once headed the Triad. I was the Dragon Master and Tsang my enforcer. It was the reason I was able to step down and how I created the legitimate Tong.

But I did not do any of that until after I lost your mother. You see I thought I could have it all. I could be the man she needed, a father to you, and we could be a family. I loved your mother and I love you so much. But the Triad, the way of life, was all I knew, and I did not want it to touch either of you. I kept the violence away from you both as much as possible. Your mother knew I was involved in the Triad, but not at what level, and certainly not that I headed the organization that covered quite a bit of the East Coast and part of the West. I am not proud of some of the things I have done and I have in my own way tried to atone.

What you do not know is your mother died because of me. Some would say it was the debt I had to pay for all the wrong I had done. But you and your mother should not have had to pay that price. It was not a random shooting. But because of the changes I was trying to make within the

Triad. When I attempted to steer us away from parts of the business, I was seen as weak by others. Liu's father placed a hit on me in a bid to take over everything. They came after me. Your mother was with me and would not leave my side. She refused to leave the store when they entered. She wanted me to go with her. To just walk away. I could not, so I fought. And I lost. She died that day and I almost did, too. Tsang stopped Liu's father and saved me.

After your mother's death I stepped down and that was when the Tong was fully born, made up of a small group of legitimate business associations. I refused to touch any of the illegal ventures. I turned everything I had been doing into legitimate concerns or turned it completely over to the Triad. Others joined me. The remaining Triad leads agreed to let me develop the Tong. As long as I remained a part of the five and paid for the privilege of keeping the Tong. With my acceptance that Liu would take his father's place. We five would then rule without a dragon's head. I was tired of the killing and only wanted peace so I agreed. For almost twenty years, I continued to develop and solidify legal businesses. But when the others saw what you were capable of, your skills, they wanted to make you part of the Triad, to ensure I would never leave. That they'd continue to benefit from the profits of the Tong. I refused.

I have left you all of my controlling interest in the Tong. Uncle Tsang will take you to the lawyers who have all the documents and handle the accounts as soon as possible. It's all yours, Maze. All I ask is that you help the Tong. Help the organization and all the businesses it represents of good people who want to do things the right way. People who I help, who help each other, to make sure the Triad does not take their hard work away from them, does not drag them into the violence that exists there. Please forgive me.

Love, Joe.

P.S. I have always been so very proud of you. You are the son of my heart. Be happy with Ivy. She loves you. Do not make my mistakes.

Uncle Tsang's voice broke through my heavy breathing. Silent tears trailed a path down my cheeks as I read Joe's last words to me.

"He left you everything, Maze," Tsang said. "And it's a lot. More than you realize. He never lived within his means. Not even Liu really knows how vast Joe's holding are, which are now yours. You are one extremely wealthy young man."

"I don't give a fuck about the money." I was breathing hard. I rubbed my hand over my face to wipe away the tears I couldn't seem to stop shedding. My body felt drained like

I'd just had the fight of my life and I lost. I was no longer numb. Rage now burned through my veins.

"You now have a choice. You can cash out, take the money, put it elsewhere, and have nothing to do with the Tong. No connection to the Triad. Just walk away. Or you can continue to do what Joe fought all these years to do. Help others protect their small businesses. Joe loaned a lot of people money, legitimately, as a result he has ownership in most of the businesses around here. He also made several investments. He was worth billions, Maze. He built up connections in Asia while I have worked on political connections in the U.S. The Tong has financing and political backing in place now. That last fight did a lot of financial, as well as influential, damage to the others. Joe knew now was the time to break completely away from the Triad."

"What?" I knew money was never an issue because it just never was. How much of it we had I never thought about. We didn't live like kings on Wall Street but we always seemed to be able to afford whatever we needed. A few million I wouldn't have been surprised to find out about but... "Fuck. It's why they tried to kill him."

"That shot was meant for me," Tsang insisted.

I raised my head. "We both know it was for you both. Don't try to protect me anymore, Uncle Tsang, from the truth."

He drained the rest of the alcohol in his glass and so did I. "The Triad might not have known the extent of his and my holdings but they know enough, and yes, they came after us both." After he grabbed the bottle and poured more into his glass, he reached toward me to refill my glass. I let him. This time, I drank it all in one gulp.

"I will do whatever you want me to do, Maze. If you decide to walk away I will buy up as much of the Tong interest as I can but I have nowhere near the funds to buy it all. I don't have Joe's kind of power, his gifts. But..." He paused and stared hard at me. "I think you do. It's what Joe saw in you and what the others sensed. I think you can be a Dragon Master."

"What?"

"Take over the Tong, let me work with you as I did with Joe. And I will deal with the Triad."

I shook my head, then turned toward the closed door but only seeing what rested beyond it. My heart beat on that couch out there. Ivy. "Right now, Uncle Tsang, there is only one thing I want to know. Who?"

"Maze, I will handle this."

I shook my head. "Who did it?"

"Jai. But he was just following orders. You know who

wanted Joe dead."

The hate and anger filling my heart momentarily sucked the air out of my lungs so all I could do was nod. It took me a minute to control myself before I spoke. "Bullshit. Jai's errant boy had warned me. He did what he did and enjoyed it." I sighed. "I understand now how naïve I really was. When I won that fight, shit seems like a million years ago now. I thought I walked away from the Triad and all of its shit. As far as the Tong, I don't know, Uncle Tsang. I will have to think about that."

"I can help you. It was Joe's legacy to you."

"I know."

"Maze…I'm sorry."

I nodded. But Joe wasn't the only one Jai had threatened. I wondered if the pain I felt every time I inhaled would ease anytime soon knowing what I had to do. And what it could cost me.

Chapter Nine

Ivy

We sat at our little table in our place having breakfast. Just cold cereal. Neither one of us felt like cooking or takeout. Maze had been withdrawn, quiet for the last few days. I couldn't blame him. We'd laid the man to rest who had been both mother and father to him for most of his life just four days ago. I hated to leave Maze.

"Are you sure?" I insisted. "I can wait until the day of the surgery and fly in then with you. You need me now."

We'd been talking about this for a couple of days now. Maze had been even more adamant that I not change my plans and still leave in the morning. Bev was having her surgery in two days, and we still had furniture being delivered, he needed to setup. But I knew Maze continued to grieve, and would for a long time.

Maze leaned over and kissed my forehead. "I'll be fine for a couple of days. Your mom and Bev need you there, and you need to be there. I'll fly down the day of the surgery. I won't be good company right now and I'd just be in the way before the surgery anyway. I know you want to spend some time with your family and friends."

"No, you won't. And you'd be fine." But he was right. He was dealing with his own issues right now coming to terms with Joe's death, but I wanted him there so I decided to tell him so. "Come for me then."

His lips curled up slightly, but no pleasure lit up his eyes. This was not the grin I'd become used to seeing from my Maze, and it killed me to find him like this. Like something inside him had died when Joe and Terry were laid to rest. Truth be told, I was scared shitless for Maze after what happened. He didn't have to tell me the shooting was Triad related. This was no random drive by but an outright assassination. I wanted him away from all of this mess and any danger.

"I will be there for you when you need me," he insisted. "Go be with your parents for a couple of days like you wanted. I'm going to use the time to finish packing the house in Brooklyn."

"Okay. Just promise me you'll be safe."

He pushed the hair that had fallen in front of my face behind my ear. "No worries."

We'd been moving Joe and Maze's things to our new

place. While Maze traveled light, Joe didn't. Maze was putting most of his stepfather's stuff in storage. Today we were going over to Dante's condo to move the rest of my stuff. Dante hadn't been happy when I told him last week I was moving out, but in the same breath I also told him Maze's stepdad had been killed. Dante had even come to the funeral. I loved my friend for that. For making that kind of effort for Maze and for me, for someone he didn't know.

Maze pulled his phone out and sent a text. He looked up at me and asked, "You ready?"

"Yeah." That's another thing. We never took cabs anywhere. With my foot still in a cast I wasn't complaining about door-to-door limo service, though. I didn't really want to question why Will, our bodyguard and Terry's replacement remained with us, and sometimes Mark. I missed Terry and I knew he'd died protecting Joe. I hadn't questioned Maze for the reasons behind the shooting. But I was scared for Maze and part of me really didn't want to know the details. This was probably very cowardly of me. Yet, another part of me needed to know if Maze was in danger.

"Do we still need a bodyguard?" I asked.

Maze stood and grabbed our cereal bowls. "It's just a precaution until Joe's murderer is caught." He turned around at the sink and rinsed out the bowls before placing them in the dishwasher.

"Do the police have any leads?" I got up and lifted my bag from the corner. We'd both given statements to the police that day at the hospital and a detective had shown up at the funeral. Maze and Mr. Tsang spoke to him while I waited in the limo with Will. There were at least three hundred people at the funeral for his stepdad. Including the Mayor of New York, and a member of Congress. Even the newspaper ran a brief story on the prominent Chinese businessman who was respected in the U.S. and Asia. The only thing is the article stated it was a drive-by shooting between rival Chinese gangs and his stepdad and driver had gotten caught in the crossfire. Given what little Maze told me, I knew it for a lie. Joe was the target.

"Nothing so far." He came over to me and stopped to take my hand in his. "Let's get the rest of your stuff so you're good and truly moved in here."

I looked into his beautiful stormy eyes. "Are you safe, Maze? Is it safe for you?"

He pulled me into a brief hug. "Hey, don't worry about me. I'll be fine. I promise."

"All right. Let's go." I had no choice but to trust him. And pray to God he was in no danger from whoever had killed Joe.

****

I still had my key to the condo and used it to open the door. I'd already texted Dante to warn him Maze and I were on the way over. I didn't want to risk walking in on him again butt naked on the couch with anyone. Although I was curious as to who it could be since he told me he and Christy weren't sleeping together any more. As soon as we stepped into the place, I saw my ex-roommate sitting at the kitchen counter. I was surprised to find him there. I glanced around and he seemed to be alone.

"Hey," I said. "I thought you'd be at class."

He looked at the clock on the microwave. "Don't have to leave for another couple of hours. It was rescheduled for later today."

"'Sup," Maze said, nodding at him.

"Hey, man. Thought I'd stick around in case you needed some help since Ivy here isn't real mobile."

"Thanks, man," Maze replied.

I chuckled. "Yeah. Thanks."

"*And* I also stuck around because I wanted to tell you in person about an opportunity to chorography some work for RBA." Dante grinned.

"What!" I squealed.

"What's that?" Maze asked looking at me.

"The Regional Ballet Association. It's made up of fifty of the top dance schools in the country. Sometimes foreign schools are a part of it. Once a year they get together for a weeklong festival. Some world famous dancers and choreographers teach classes to the best of these students. The last two nights there are about ten performances in front of a crowd of roughly a thousand. The schools all compete to have their dancers and original choreography chosen to be showcased those last two nights. Out of the fifty schools only maybe ten are chosen to give special performances that can bring more students into the school, provide scholarships, and offers of professional contracts."

Maze smiled. "So this is a big deal."

"Damn straight," Dante said. "We've taught couples classes before and have been asked to do it again, but this time my old dance school wants us to choreograph something for them."

To be asked to chorography a piece like this was quite a coup, but not for me. "My foot, Dante. I can't dance."

"You know you don't need to. These are advanced dance students. You only have to explain the necessary movement and concept. I can demonstrate the pattern without you. And you don't have to move for us to come up with a dance piece together."

I shook my head. "You'd still need to practice with a partner."

He shrugged. "So we can work out the basics on paper then once we get to the school we can work out the practicality with the dancers."

I chewed my bottom lip. "I don't know."

Maze, who'd never left my side, leaned against the counter. He placed his arm around my waist and rested his chin on my shoulder. "I do. You can do this, Ivy. I believe in you." His attention moved to Dante. "When do you have to do this by, man?"

"This week would be good to start planning but I know you have to go home, Ivy, so after you get back, we can get to work. Then in a couple of weeks the two of us would fly to Philly where I went to school and spend two weeks there with the dancers. The festival is in six weeks."

"She'll do it," Maze said before I could reply.

I twisted and glanced at him. "Hey, I haven't agreed to this."

"But you will," Dante said.

He was right. In my heart, I was a dancer, and yes we did some chorography on the side and some pieces for the show so it wouldn't be too hard to choreograph something for this competition. And if the piece was chosen to be presented that would be huge for us. Suddenly, I didn't feel quite so hopeless that I might not be able to perform professionally again. I wasn't yet twenty-two, I still had a good five years left, if my ankle held up. But creating movement, interpreting music was something else I loved. The opportunity was another way for me to continue doing what I enjoyed most. Dance. But it meant being away from Maze.

"Are you sure?" I asked Maze.

He shook his head. "Yep, and you guys can meet down at the gym if you need to. There's a room you can use."

I snickered and both men stared at me.

"What's so funny?" Maze asked frowning.

I raised one hand and waved it in front of my face. Shaking my head at the same time not ready to tell them yet.

Dante looked at Maze and shrugged. I laughed again. I couldn't help it. "I...I just thought of Dante wearing his tights in a room full of MMA fighters."

Maze cracked up. It had been a week since I heard the sound of his laughter. Dante sat up in his chair. The look of horror on his face ensured my mirth wouldn't stop just then.

"I am not fucking wearing tights to the fucking gym!"

Dante growled.

"I will if you will," I grinned.

Maze stopped laughing. "Oh, hell no."

I snorted. After the week we had it felt good to laugh. I loved him for that.

Maze's phone pinged like he had a text. He pulled it out and looked at it. "Listen, I gotta run a quick errand since I'm on this side of town."

"What? Where are you going?" I asked.

"I won't be long and I'll be back before Dante has to leave. Stay here."

Maze pressed his lips to mine and just like that he was gone. I turned around to find Dante staring at me.

"What's that about?" Dante inquired.

"I don't know." I hobbled into my bedroom. Dante followed me, bringing the three boxes in Maze had brought up with him.

Dante dropped them on the floor by my closet door. "Well something's going on, Ivy. I can't help but think that whatever happened to Maze's stepdad has something to do with that underground fighting ring he's a part of."

Even Dante figured that much out. But what could I say to him? I didn't want to lie to my friend. Then again I wasn't sure what was going on. I only had my suspensions, but I would not betray Maze or Joe. However, I could relieve Dante's concerns about one thing. "Maze is no longer involved in professional fighting. The fight you saw was his last one. He now owns that gym in Chinatown he was talking about us training in, and the apartment we're moving into is on the top floor. He owns it. He's just going to train new fighters. Provide a place for them. That's it." I grabbed a bunch of jackets and passed them to him.

Dante frowned as he took the stack from me. He folded and placed them in the box. "Are you sure he's done?"

I nodded.

"Still, I'm worried about you. Whatever happened was no accident."

"I'm fine. You don't need to worry."

"But I do, you know. I don't want you caught up in any shit he's involved in. You know I respect him but I care about you more. And if you ever need me all you have to do is call and I'm a cab ride away. Your room will always be available."

I turned and placed my hand on his sleeve and he drew me in for a tight hug. The embrace lasted longer than it should have. His fingers dug into me, like he didn't want to let go and his breathing came out a little ragged. "I'm going to miss you," he whispered against my hair.

I pulled away, and looked at him, it was then I saw the yearning in his gaze. Maze had been right. Dante had feelings for me. Maybe they had been there all along. I'd just been blind. "Dante…I'm sorry…I…"

He placed his finger over my lips. "It's okay. I know you've made your choice. And I will always be your best friend. Now let's finish getting you packed up."

I was floored. I had no idea that our connection for him went beyond deep friendship. On my part I only loved him as a friend. When we'd first met I thought his flirting had been mere teasing. He practically flirted with everyone, and then after we became roommates, he stopped and we'd become best friends. I told him all about Maze. So Dante always understood, my heart and soul belonged to Maze. They had from the first time I'd ever laid eyes on him. So I smiled at my friend. "I do love you, you know."

"Yeah. I know."

"Just not…"

"Shhh. I know that, too."

I didn't want to lose Dante. I smiled sadly at him and grabbed another handful of clothes and handed them to him.

****

I couldn't talk Maze into coming with me, and it was so

hard to leave him.

"It's just two days, babe," he'd said. "And then I'll be there. I'll come straight from the airport to the hospital."

"I wish neither one of us had to make this trip. I wish it was just a regular visit home."

"Me too, babe." He'd wrapped his arm around me and kissed my forehead just before he walked me to the security area. He could go with me no farther.

It was good to be home, though. I spoke and texted with my folks all the time but I hadn't seen my dad in months. Mom picked me up from the airport, but Dad came home early so he was there when I got home. I was so pampered. Came from being an only child I supposed. My dad was a couple inches taller than Maze and swallowed me in his embrace.

"How's my girl?" he bellowed. He had a deep voice, which I loved.

"Find, Daddy." Both my parents had a little gray threaded through their hair but were still in good shape for forty-something year olds. I looked like a younger version of my mom. She was maybe a size larger than I was. Dad liked to brag he could still fit into the suit he got married in, but he had a little tummy now. Which he blamed on my mom's great cooking.

"I hear you have a boyfriend now." He looked behind me like he was looking for someone. "I'm surprised he's not with you," he laughed.

I knew he was kidding around, although I was sure Mom told him Maze was more than just a friend. He wouldn't expect him to come home with me. I never brought boys home, aside from Dante a couple of times, but he was just a friend.

"Ah, he's coming the morning of Bev's surgery. I already let Mom know." I spoke the last hurriedly.

My dad frowned. "Why? He doesn't have a reason to be there."

"Phil," my mom said lightly swatting his arm. "Obviously he's coming to support Ivy."

I'd told my mom about Maze visiting. I guess she forgot to tell my dad. "Yeah, Dad. Remember he also knew Shel. He knows how much the Stevensons mean to me."

Dad frowned. "Fine. I guess it's only for one night. He can sleep in the basement."

"Thank you." It's not like I ever dated much. Dancing was a jealous master. I had only a handful of boyfriends. None lasted more than a couple of months. Even when I was a teenager and lived at home.

I kissed my parents then went up to my room. My dad

got a phone call and Mom carried my bag up the stairs for me. As soon as we got to my room, she closed the door. I sat on the bed. Not sure what was going on but clearly she wanted to talk.

She put the case down and sat on the bed next to me. "How's Maze holding up?"

Mom and Dad had sent Maze a card and flowers to the cemetery.

"He's doing okay. It's hard sometimes though."

"That's understandable," she said. "And the fact he's coming to be here with you now says a lot about him. So are you two serious?"

This was it. I hadn't told my folks Maze and I had moved in together. My dad almost had a cow when he first found out I'd be living with Dante, but when he heard he was a dancer he relaxed. That and the fact I insisted we were just friends. Separate rooms he could deal with. Maze and I did not have separate anything.

"Yes. I think so. Mom, I have something to tell you but you can't tell Dad yet. I don't want him to freak."

She laid her hand over mine. "What is it, honey?"

I took a deep breath, and then exhaled. "Maze and I moved in together a few days ago."

She squeezed my hand and took a deep breath. "I see.

And are you sure about this?"

"Yes. I'm sure, Mom."

She glanced away then back at me, this time putting both hands over mine. "I'm not going to say I approve. I'm assuming when you say 'moved in' you're not talking about the way you lived with Dante."

I shook my head.

She sighed. "You are an adult now, honey, even though you're both so young. But in truth, you've been on your own living in New York for a long time. I've stopped telling you what to do ages ago, so I can't really start now. I let you live your dream." She smiled. "But given your determination to become a professional dancer I'm not sure I could have stopped you either. And as a result you're an accomplished beautiful ballerina but...tell me this: do you love him?"

I nodded, my eyes tearing up at the thought of my love for Maze.

"Does he feel the same way?"

Again, I nodded unable to speak.

She tilted her head. "I trust your judgment and I'm happy for both of you. But I expect this to be a temporary situation and something more permanent to develop sooner rather than later."

"Mom!"

She put up her hands in the air. "Don't 'Mom' me, hon. If you're going to commit, then commit all the way that's all I'm saying."

"I'll take that under advisement."

"See that you do. Now what about your ankle and dance?"

"I've still got several weeks before the cast comes off but in the meantime I'm going to do some chorography with Dante. We've been asked to do a piece to present for Regional."

"Honey, that's fantastic!" She hugged me then pulled back. "I'm so proud of you. I know you guys are going to win."

My mom knew the importance of Regional; she'd taken me to quite a few of them when I was younger.

"When and where is it? Dad and I would love to come and so would Bev and Ben."

"I'll send you the details if our piece gets chosen."

"Of course, your piece will be chosen. They'd be crazy not to include anything you and Dante come up with. Your work together is brilliant. So is this what you're going to do from now on? I thought you were also going to work on strengthening your ankle so you could dance again."

I nodded, feeling more optimistic about everything.

"Yep. I'll be doing that, too. As soon as the cast comes off I'll begin exercising it. Maze already says he's got plans for me, specific exercises he's going to have me do.

"That's what he'd mentioned at dinner. I knew I liked that boy. You'll be up on pointe again in no time."

"From your ears to the ankle god's mouth."

She leaned forward and hugged me. "Okay, brat. Let me go fix dinner. Pasta cabonara sound good?"

"Perfect." Yeah, it was good to be home.

My phone chimed just as my mom closed my door. I had a text. I got my phone out of my bag.

Maze: *'You get there okay?'*

Ivy: *'Yep. It's all good.'*

Maze: *'Miss you.'*

Ivy: *'Miss you, too'*

Maze: *'Have a good night. I Love you.'*

Ivy: *'Love you too. Mwah!'*

Maze: *'xoxoxo'*

I put my phone down and went downstairs for dinner. I missed my parents but it was always good to be home. I was glad when my mom kept the conversation away from Maze and me and focused it on Bev and things going on with mutual friends. The last thing I wanted to do was discuss my living arrangements with Maze. I got out of doing dishes and went upstairs to get ready for bed. After I hung up my clothes so they wouldn't wrinkle, I picked up my cell again and called Maze. I just wanted to hear his voice before falling asleep.

I got under the covers and opened my list of favorite numbers. The phone rang once and went straight to voice mail. I frowned a little disappointed that I couldn't reach him, but left him a message. "I just wanted to hear your voice before I fell asleep. I love you. Good night."

Chapter Ten

Maze

Lightning flashed over the wing. The way the area lit up, I could have sworn the bolt struck the plane but it didn't do any damage. At least none I could see. The flight during a thunderstorm was not a smooth one but finally I landed at Ronald Reagan Airport in Washington D.C. After last night, I wondered if storms were now going to rule my life.

I shivered. Cold. So fucking cold, and it had nothing to do with the weather. Everything changed two nights ago. I took no pleasure in what I'd done, I almost didn't get on the plane earlier this morning. Feeling unworthy of Ivy. But I've always felt unworthy of her. Like she was this diamond and I was well, anything but, and now…

I looked down at my hands. There was no blood visible, but I could still see the crimson there. And feared there would be more.

Ivy needed me by her side today, and I would be there. I just didn't know for how much longer. As I walked out of the terminal and caught a cab to the hospital my only thought was I would do all I could to make damn sure Ivy remained safe.

I glanced out the window and saw lightning light up the gray sky across the water. The rain had been heavy even before I left JFK. When the bolt flashed, it brought to mind the memory of the flash of Jai's blade striking against my own. He let me gaze upon his hatred for me stamped on his face, his determination to see me dead. In the end, I also witnessed his acceptance of his own death when my knife sliced across his throat. I don't think I'd ever experience a storm again and not think of how my life had changed.

I pulled out my phone and texted Ivy I was there. I just needed to get to her. At least I came alone. Uncle Tsang didn't want me to travel without Will but after what went down, Joe's death and then Jai's, the Triad wasn't doing anything for a while. Tsang wasn't too happy with what I'd done either. I'd gotten the information I wanted without involving him. The day I left Ivy with Dante I'd gone to a popular fight hang out and found out where Jai was going to be the next night. The message I sent to the Triad was loud and clear. I understood Tsang's fear that I would be unprotected, but our enemies didn't know who Ivy was. It would take time to find out her information and then to figure out where I'd gone. By then we'd be back in New York surrounded by Tong where the Triad couldn't touch us.

Yesterday I'd signed all the paperwork with the lawyers, and then met with some of the business owners. I now owned the primary shares in the Tong. A conglomerate of business interests spanning the gambit from restaurants, retail stores, dry cleaners, even a few small IT and software companies. All of which I didn't know fuck about. Almost twenty-four years old and I had businessmen who'd run successful companies for years looking up to me. *Crap!* I had a shitload to learn and no time to learn it. First and foremost the Triad had to go. Really just Liu. Cut off the head of a snake and the rest will die. This shit began with the deaths of his father and my mother. It was time for it to end. I hoped it ended with Jai's death but that could be just wishful thinking on my part.

I got out of the cab in front of the hospital entrance. The last song playing in the cab ride over resonated in my soul. Yeah, I was knee deep in Coolio's *Gangsta's Paradise*. Right down to the fucking snakes. I took a deep breath to shake out the depressing thoughts. I had a woman to face who needed me strong and focused on her. I only carried a backpack with a change of clothes. I didn't need much. I was there for Ivy. As soon as I stepped through the sliding doors

I walked toward the reception desk. It didn't escape my notice I'd been spending an awful lot of time in hospitals lately. Creeped me the hell out. The sound of my name had me swinging in another direction, and there was my girl hurrying to me. I smiled for the first time in days and opened my arms. She hobbled right into them, I picked her up, and covered her lips to mine.

God, I missed her. I wrapped my arms around her tighter. She was my anchor. My light. Her warmth rushed through my veins breaking the ice. I prayed to God she never found out what I was capable of doing. What I had done. When I thought I could breathe on my own I put her down.

"Well, I guess that means you're happy to see me," I joked.

She smiled. "Yeah." She grabbed my elbow. "How was the flight? I'm sorry the weather is so crappy."

"It was fine. No worries."

"Come on. Bev's being prepped now."

I followed her to the elevator. I would have kissed her again but a woman and a toddler got on with us. When the elevator opened, we got off and walked down a hallway past a nurse's station. Ivy led me into another section but it was kinda crowded. It looked more like a prepping area cause only curtains separated one room from another. I recognized

Bev's husband and Ivy's mom. A tall handsome medium brown skinned man had his hands on Allison's shoulders. Ivy's dad. A doctor and nurse stood near the bed. We stayed in the general area.

"Hey, everyone. Look who I found," Ivy said.

"Hi." I sent out the greeting to everyone. I felt uncomfortable as hell when all those parental gazes swung my way. Not something I was used to. But I gotta give Ivy's mom props. She stepped away from her husband and came over to me to give me a hug. Shocked the shit outta me.

"How you holding up?" she asked, looking up into my eyes.

"I'm good."

When she stepped back Ben came over and shook my hand. "It's good to see you again, Maze."

"You too," I replied.

"Dad," Ivy said looking at her father, "Do you remember Maze?"

"Sure. How are you, son? I'm sorry for your loss." Her dad stepped forward and shook my hand, too.

"Thank you, sir." Oh fuck, fuck. I had to use everything I'd ever learned to keep my breathing even and not hyperventilate like I wanted to. I could weld a steel blade and draw blood with ice in my veins but meeting these people freaked my shit out. These were the adults in Ivy's life. They meant something to her. I could do this.

I glanced over at Ivy. *For her. All for her.*

Bev waved at me when the doctor stepped aside. "Thanks for coming, Maze."

"No problem, Bev."

"It's time," the nurse said.

Ivy released my hand and went over to the bed. She kissed Bev on her cheek. "Love you, Aunt Bev," she said. "We'll be here when you wake up."

She came back over to me and took my hand. "Come on." She turned to her parents. "We're going down to the cafeteria. We'll meet you back at the waiting area. Do you need anything?"

They shook their heads.

I took a deep breath when we walked away. We located the cafeteria, which also had an open atrium area. I wasn't really hungry and neither was Ivy. We got a couple of hot teas and found a secluded area. A bistro table for two tucked into a corner. I scooted the chair even closer so we were seated side by side and faced the rest of the room. I looked up. The roof had a skylight in the center, but it was an awful day so all I could see was water making a losing bid to get inside.

Ivy looked up, too. "I know. Like I said, crappy day."

I held her hand. "Any day someone's having surgery is a crappy day."

"Thank you so much for being here with me."

I raised her hand to my mouth and my lips met her knuckles. "Where else would I be but by your side when you need me?"

"How are you holding up?" she asked.

Somehow I managed to dredge up a smile for her. "Better now that I'm with you." I reached over and wrapped one arm around her shoulder and she leaned her head on me.

"I missed you," she said.

"I doubt anywhere as much as I missed you. You know for the last few weeks the last couple of nights were the first time I haven't woken up with you in my arms. I'm not sure I got any sleep." And it was true. For so many reasons.

She leaned back to look at me. "And we won't be sleeping together tonight either. Dad's relegated you to the basement."

I winched. But wasn't all that surprised. "Why?"

"Because they're parents."

"Okay, okay but I miss you." And I did. I'd missed her so much already and wouldn't have her with me tonight. I needed to hold her in my arms. Skin to skin. I badly wanted to bury myself in her essence and feel a measure of sanity again.

She chuckled. "It's just one more night and we'll be home tomorrow."

"I like the way you think. Yeah, home. Have you told your folks we moved in together?" She was not quick to answer. "Ivy…"

"Ah, I told my mom. She's not excited about it but she's cool with it. She understands how much we love each other."

"Okay, and your dad?"

She shook her head. "I haven't told him yet."

"Why?"

She sat up trying to put a little distance between us but I wasn't having any of that.

I pulled her back into my embrace. "Why haven't you?" I asked again.

"He's my dad, Maze. He had a fit when he first found out I'd be living with Dante. Then once he realized he was gay, well bi, but Dad thinks he's gay. Anyway he relented. Especially when he came to visit and saw we had separate bedrooms and bathrooms."

"Okay. So tell him about us. Are you ashamed of me?"

God say no. But maybe she should be. I still didn't understand what the hell she saw in someone like me. There was nothing refined about me. The only time I listened to classical music was if it was in a commercial or a movie score. I wouldn't know the difference between a salad fork, dessert fork, and entree fork. I've used chopsticks most of my life. I'm not even sure I can have a normal conversation with someone for half an hour and not slip a shit, damn, or fuck in there. Lunch with Ivy's mom and friends was hellish in that respect. I barely spoke.

She cocked her head to the side. "No, no that's not it. I just want my dad to get to know you a little first. To understand how much we care for each other before I tell him. And I will. Just not this visit, okay? Do you get why?"

"Yeah, I do." No way in fuck was her father ever going to approve of some tattooed fighter shacking up with his baby girl. I know if we ever had a daughter I'd kill the sonofabitch who tried that shit. *Whoa.* Where did that thought come from? On the one hand the possibility scared the crap outta me, on the other, it excited me. But then reality had me crashing back down to earth. The clock was ticking for us. Ivy deserved to be with someone who could truly keep her safe and away from the violence dogging my life. My mood headed for the deep end of the tank again.

"Oh I spoke to my doctor and he wants me to come in, in a few weeks. I might get my cast off then and wrap it up or get a walking cast."

"That's great news."

"Yeah. So after I get back from Philly I might be able to get this damn thing off and we can begin exercising my ankle."

"That's good, babe. But only if the doctor says it's okay. So when do you leave?" I'd forgotten about the project she was doing with Dante. Even though Dante and I had made peace we'd never be best friends. I knew the minute I left he'd be right there to pick up the pieces. I couldn't blame him and I knew he'd be good to her. Was better for her. Didn't matter, though. She was mine. And I was not giving her up until the very last second I had to. Because I loved her enough to want her safe from any fallout shit. The fact she'd be gone for a couple of weeks would be a good thing. Regardless of the emptiness I already felt at the thought of being apart from her for so long.

We returned to the waiting area and sat with her parents for a while and then they left us to grab something to eat, forcing Ben to go with them. Eventually they came back and shortly thereafter the doctor returned to talk to us. Ivy and I remained seated and her parents stood on either side of Ben. Her mom held his hand while her dad had his on Ben's shoulder, silently offering him their presence and their support before the doctor gave them the results. Their unwavering unity punched a hole in my gut. These were good people. They cared about each other. *This* was Ivy's world and it was normal. There were no bodyguards. No one tried to screw you over or kill you because of a business deal or because they wanted to protect their illegal trade. Just normal. I looked down at Ivy's hand enclosed in mine. She squeezed me and I looked up at her.

"What's wrong?" she asked.

"Nothing. Your parents and Ben and Bev are great people."

"Yes, they are and they've accepted you as an important part of my life, too."

"You think so?"

"Yes."

Little did they know.

We weren't near enough to hear everything the doctor told them but we heard some of it and from the way everyone's shoulders relaxed it seemed like good news. Allison turned to us and smiled. "She's going to be fine kids. They got it all."

Ivy jumped up and rushed to her family, embracing everyone. They stood there crying and holding onto each other.

Yeah, normal. I never felt more like an outsider watching them. The love and care they had for each other was palpable. Joe and I loved each other but we'd never really been the touchy sort until he landed in the hospital. These people showed affection like that all the time. I'm glad I had that brief kind of time with Joe, to tell him I loved him. It wasn't till Ivy entered my life I even became aware of the different types of intimacy existing between people. Love and loyalty yes, but this was somehow different. What I saw before me I'd never been a part of. But then Ivy, my amazing Ivy, looked up and held out her hand to me. Unable to stop myself, I got up and grasped it like my life depended on it. She enclosed me in the circle. But in my heart I was well aware she couldn't save me. It was too late.

Chapter Eleven

Ivy

I lay on my side facing Maze and watching him sleep. God he took my breath away. I smiled. Such a stupid thing to think a person could be responsible for every breath you take, but nonetheless true. Cause he was. But something was wrong. I thought at first it had to do with Joe's death, but ever since we'd gotten back from Maryland there was something forced about Maze. Like he tried to distance himself from me, from us. He was still demonstrative and loving, he'd still kiss me or hold my hand every chance he got but at night, at night he'd just hold me and fall asleep. I knew he spent most of his days in the gym.

The new equipment had come and been installed and he'd been trying everything out. Developing an exercise routine for some of the new fighters he'd already taken on. And he even had me down there doing some upper body and core exercises. He was right, it did feel good to exercise. Even if I couldn't do anything that put weight on my foot.

He explained about some of the exercises he'd have me do once the cast was off and it made perfect sense. I actually began to believe I might have a shot. While thanks to Maze I felt optimistic about my future as a dancer, but underneath it all a thread of sadness ran through our relationship. I couldn't put my finger on the cause only that it was there. Yet, we were happy together. I knew we were. He kissed and touched me every chance he got. There were times I'd feel eyes on me and look up to find him staring at me, and he'd wink or smile. But we'd been back from my parents for the last five days and we hadn't made love.

Maze who couldn't keep his hands off me or let me keep my hands off him was too tired at night. He'd either fall into bed before I got there or long after I'd fallen asleep, and all he'd want to do was sleep. In the morning he'd usually be up before me and down in the gym.

I'd leave in a couple of days for Philly with Dante and I aimed to change whatever held him back tonight.

Maze lay on his side facing me but when I shifted out of his embrace he rolled onto his back, one arm flung straight out. I pulled off my t-shirt but left my boxer-style underwear on. I watched as his chest rose and fell. His breathing even, he slept on.

Not for long.

I scooted farther down his torso, pulling the covers up and off of him as I moved. I smiled as his body was revealed to me even though parts of him lay in shadows on the mattress. I could see enough of his shape to tell his dick lay placid against him. One leg rested stretched straight out and the other curled up.

I made my way to the space he'd left open in the center. Lowering my head, I tasted him from base to tip. His dick pulsed. I kissed the mushroom top and it jumped to full life. I licked around the head before taking him into my mouth. He groaned, spreading his legs wider to give me easier access.

"Ivy," he breathed.

"Mmm…" was all I could manage as I knelt before him and took him deeper into my mouth. Loving his texture, the size of him filling my mouth. His taste. Loving the pleasure I drew from him every time he groaned. He flexed his hips in rhythm with my movements. Pushing himself farther into my throat until I took all of him in. I wrapped one hand around his balls and his stem to hold him steady, while I sucked him off. His fingers moved and grasped my other hand that lay on the bed beside him. He entwined our fingers and squeezed as I worked him. I lifted my mouth off him and removed my hand from his so I could mount him. I still held him within my grasp, while he held on to my waist and guided me over his wet shaft. I slid him slowly into me and moaned.

Our breaths came in and out in sync.

His chest rose and fell. His eyes were halfway closed but they were aimed on the space where we were joined. "Ride me, baby. Take me with you."

And I did. I placed my palms on his chest and felt the vibration of his heart through my fingers all the way to my soul. He pulsed for me inside and out. He grasped my hands and I gripped him with my inner muscles to hold him inside of me. Continuing to hold onto his hands, I leaned back until my back almost touched the mattress between his legs. All the while he pushed into me.

"Damn, girl." Maze moaned.

Using nothing but pure core strength he pulled us both up until we were face to face. I sat on his lap with him still buried deep inside of me. My arms wrapped around his neck. He buried his face in the center of my tits and kissed both sides before wrapping one hand around my waist. With his other hand, he gripped the back of my head and plastered our mouths together as he erupted inside of me and I drenched him in my cum.

He stopped kissing me but his lips hovered over mine.

His words came out more as a breath. "I love you. I need you to know that. I love you and always will."

"I love you, too."

He lifted me slightly until his dick rested calm between us. I looked down at him. I could barely see him in the dark and smiled. I rolled off him and onto the bed. He got up and walked into the bathroom. I heard the water go on in there and then he came out with a wash cloth. It was warm and he proceeded to clean between my legs. It was one of the sweetest things he'd ever done and I wanted him again. He dropped the washcloth on the floor and climbed back up on the bed. Face to face he used his knee to nudge my leg apart so he could move his leg between mine. He rested one arm under my neck the other across my hip. Leaning forward he kissed my nose. "Sleep, baby."

"Maze?"

"Yeah?"

"Are we okay? Are you okay?"

"Yeah."

I wanted to believe him, I did. But his face was engulfed in shadows and I couldn't see his eyes. I wanted to believe he was still just grieving for Joe. It took me a long time to get over Shelly's death. To function normally. So maybe all Maze needed was a little more time. And a lot of love. So I scooted even closer and he tightened his embrace. I closed my eyes, and let sleep and the feeling of safety I got from being in his arms surround me.

****

Two weeks without my Maze. I'm not sure how I survived it. He'd flown out once to see me in Philly but only for two days. It would be difficult for me to navigate on one or even two crutches through the airport, and he refused to have me do so. This sucked, and even when he was here he seemed distant. But wouldn't tell me what was up. I was miserable. I enjoyed what Dante and I had accomplished with the group of young and talented dancers. The problem came when I was alone, missing Maze, and the thoughts I could no longer keep out of my mind pushed to the surface.

Before I'd left New York we made love several times. Morning, noon, and night. He even corned me in the private room he'd set aside for Dante and me to practice in. He had mirrors put in and a ballet bar. He'd put in a wooden floor so we could do pointe. The day the installation was finished he took me in there and shut and locked the door. The next thing I knew he had me on the floor watching us in the mirror as we made love. I get hot for him just thinking about it. Picturing him gliding in and out of me, his flesh wet with my essence. All the while we watched each other in the mirror.

I left him in New York thinking things were better now. That he was better and the worst of his grief put behind us. But when he'd come to Philly I wasn't so sure. Again I couldn't put my finger on the problem, and when I asked him about what was bothering him, he insisted everything was fine.

I sat on the flight next to Dante, on my way back to New York, with a lot of thoughts swirling in my mind. Maze would pick me up at the airport tonight, and I wanted this settled once and for all, whatever was going on with him. Ever since Joe's death he'd distanced himself from me and I couldn't stand it anymore.

Earlier that morning Dante showed me an article on his *iPad*. It was about two deaths that occurred in Chinatown recently. The reason it stuck with me was because I recognized the picture of one of the dead men the article talked about. He was the guy at the rooftop bar that night. The one who tried to egg Maze into a fight. He'd been beheaded by a sharp object. But the thing that had my heart racing was the rest of the article. His death might be linked to another that occurred two weeks before. Both men were known to have ties to the local Triad and the article speculated the deaths were related to a turf war. Which was why Dante showed it to me. I did not want to believe Maze knew anything about it. He had nothing to do with the Triad any more. Thank God! But what if he were in danger of some kind? What if he could have been one of those guys killed because of this war? Was he a target? I had to know.

After we exited the passenger only area of the airport, we took the escalator down to baggage claim. I saw a familiar face at the bottom of the steps. I missed him so much.

I walked right into Maze's arms and he pressed his lips to mine. We were so wrapped up in each other it wasn't until I heard Dante's voice saying, "For Christ sake get a room," that I pulled away and realized we were blocking the path.

"Hey, man," Maze said by way of greeting to Dante. He took the carryon I held out of my hand and placed the strap over his shoulder, then took my hand in his.

"Come on let's go." He turned and led the way to the baggage claim area. Dante walked on the other side of me as I hobbled along.

"How was the flight?" Maze asked.

"It was good," I said.

"Yeah, not bad for a puddle jumper," Dante quipped.

"I'd have gotten you first class tickets but most of the non-stop flights are on the smaller planes," Maze said to me.

"It's fine. We're here now."

We grabbed our bags from the claim area and Maze called Will to let him know what arrival point to pick us up from. We didn't have long to wait before the limo pulled up and we piled into the car. Traffic wasn't too bad so we made good time into the city and stopped to drop Dante off first. I sat in the middle of the guys so I turned and gave Dante a hug before he stepped out of the car.

"I'll talk to you tomorrow and we can set up a schedule after my cast comes off," I said.

"Sounds good. Have a good evening you two," Dante said. "And don't do anything I would."

"No worries there." I laughed. God alone knew the things Dante would do.

He got out and closed the door.

I leaned back into Maze's embrace. It was going to be strange not seeing Dante every day again. We'd had a lot of fun together, just like always. I really enjoyed the chorography we came up with, and teaching was fun, too. Now I knew if I had to give up dancing professionally it would be choreography I'd peruse.

Maze circled both arms around me, hugging me tighter to him and bringing my thoughts back to him, to us. He felt so good. Yet, I couldn't quite forget the article weighing on me since I read it earlier this morning. But I didn't want to begin the conversation I knew we had to have in the car. I would wait until we got home.

I threaded my arm though his. "I missed this," I said.

"Me, too."

"Are you sorry you let me go away for so long?"

"No. I know how much it meant to you."

I twisted to glance up at him. "Thank you." I kissed the bottom of his chin, then sat back against him. "You know if they chose our piece it will be presented at the festival in less than two months and I'll be gone for two maybe three days then."

"Of course they'll choose your piece. They'd be crazy not to."

"Will you come with me?"

"I'll come the night of the performance. I'd just be in your way the rest of the time."

I turned to look at him again, shifting to make sure he could see the sincerity in my face. "You will never be in the way. I want you to come."

"We'll see. I took on a couple of fighters and one might have a fight around that time."

Fear shot down my spine. "But I thought you didn't have anything to do with that world any more?"

He shook his head. "I don't. I stay in the gym and provide training and guidance. I don't go to the fights."

"Swear to me."

"I swear. I don't go to the fights. I'll never step into another arena again."

My heart rate calmed down a little but his reply still didn't answer the questions I needed to ask.

Will pulled up in front of our building and stopped the car. Before he could come around and open the door, Maze jumped out on the other side. I saw him speak to Will before he came around to my side and opened the door for me.

Maze helped me out and Will went around to the back and got my suitcase and carryon. Maze took them from him, then opened our street door. I went in first and maneuvered up the stairs, Maze behind me. I unlocked our front door and stepped into our place. Although we hadn't lived there very long I already thought of the place as home. Maze and I had chosen all of the furniture together. The beige and peacock blue colors helped lend a comfortable feel to the place. The cozy furniture was just the kind you could sit down and relax on.

I made my way over to the long, wide couch and did just that. I dropped my purse on the coffee table and Maze came in and shut the door.

"I'll put these in the bedroom and then we can decide on dinner. You have anything in mind?" Maze asked.

"Yeah. One of us should learn to cook," I yelled back, only kidding. Thanks to Dante I knew enough to follow simple recipes.

Maze came back into the room without my things. He had an *iPad* in his hand and plopped down on the couch beside me. "Well, we can start by getting an easy recipe app, or better yet, let's see if they have cooking for dummies?" He flashed me his killer grin. The one where his dimples showed up. It had been a long time since I'd seen them.

"Speak for yourself. But seriously we don't need to try to cook anything tonight. Besides, we'd first have to go to the grocery store, then by the time we got back and fixed something it would probably be midnight. I'm hungry now."

"Take out it is then. Any preference?"

"I could go for a steak."

Maze pulled out his phone and placed an order, then put the cell on the table. He sat back and we leaned against each other.

Now was the time. "I need to ask you something."

He played with my fingers. "What is, babe?"

"I read an article today in the paper about the death of a Triad member, the same guy at the roof top bar that night that tried to get you to fight."

I felt his body tense beside me. It wasn't anything overt and if I hadn't been leaning against him and knew him so well I would not have noticed. The sensation was fleeting, but long enough not to have been my imagination.

"Yeah?"

"The paper talked about how his head was decapitated and another suspected Triad member died a couple of weeks ago. The cops think it's some sort of turf war going on. Are you in danger, Maze? Does this have anything to do with Joe's death?"

Chapter Twelve

Maze

I didn't want to answer her questions. I knew she wasn't stupid and if she found out about the deaths, she might make a leap. A right one, just not right enough. I knew about the murders, more than she realized. I was grateful for that at least.

I shook my head. I'd tried to keep all of the violence away from her but that damn Liu wouldn't let it go. Wouldn't let the Tong go without a fucking fight. The Triad was desperate. They lost a shitload of money and a lot of political ground. And all of it to the Tong. To me. Last week I'd had a business lunch with the top dozen businessmen of the Tong and it had been hammered home for me. There had even been a city councilman there. They'd all been present at Joe's funeral. I'd even met a few at some of my fights. I was surprised when the head of the small business association called me to set up the meeting and Tsang wasn't present. I'd had a similar meeting when I'd taken over ownership of the gym with some of the business owners on the block, but this was different.

It was only then I'd found out my uncle wasn't a member of the association. I shouldn't have been surprised though. Tsang walked a fine line. In truth, so did I now. But they made it clear I led the Tong and the association stood behind me. I understood at least on paper I owned a percentage or at least half of most of their businesses. What I hadn't fully appreciated was the influence I also had upon these men. I had been surprised when they handed me an additional file. I also owned a security firm. Will and Mark actually worked for the Tong business group, for me. It was good to know. These people had me put on a frigging suit and attend a business luncheon with them in my honor. Me being honored for continuing Joe's legacy. I wish Ivy could have been there with me. This war had to end and soon. I hoped Tsang was making headway.

I feared though, for Liu, it was no longer business. It had become personal. Perhaps it had always been so, ever since his father had been killed and Joe stepped down. I'd come to understand the way the Triad worked. I got drawn into the world in spite of my desire not to. But it didn't mean I would stay there. Liu thought he'd step in as head of the Triad and the Tong in its early conception. That he would be named

Dragon Master after he'd come of age and proven himself. But Joe and Tsang made damn sure that wouldn't happen. With Joe's death and the rise of the Tong now it never would, but Liu refused to accept that. The way he refused to accept Jai's death as payment for Joe's. He wanted me to be part of the Triad, to be one of them, to turn over the Tong to him, or die. None were an option.

But I could tell Ivy none of this. Not that Liu was out for my blood or that I had killed and might have to do more. I'd been deluding myself. These last couple of weeks I thought I'd be able to take care of this so when Ivy returned to New York she'd be safe. She wasn't. Liu knew we lived together, that she meant something to me. The fact she'd been gone for two weeks was good. I'd used that time to plant other ideas. That maybe she didn't. I made it a point to be seen around town with other women. I'd even brought a couple of them to the gym to watch me spar. I knew word would get back to Liu. It killed me to even be around those women. To have them touch me. To touch them to make it look at least in public that they meant nothing to me, which was true. I had to do it, though. I had to make them believe Ivy was just one of many.

The fact Ivy was no longer in the apartment helped to confirm the rouse. Took pressure off her. Then a few nights ago that asshole from the rooftop confronted me, he wanted to avenge Jai. Fucker came at me, blades drawn. I had hoped Jai would be the end of it, but knew that was wishful thinking on my part. While I killed Jai out right, because of what he did to Joe and his threat to Ivy, the other, it was either him or me. That one I had no choice. Nonetheless, blood spilled on my hands. Again.

I closed my eyes wondering not for the first or second time if I'd ever be clean again.

"Well?" Ivy asked, bringing me out of my dark musings.

I had been putting this off. Refusing to consider it, but I knew what I had to do. The pain gripping my chest hurt like a motherfucker but it had to be done. I would let no harm come to Ivy. And until I took care of Liu she would be in danger. I needed to get her out of here. I needed it to look like she truly was nothing more than another piece of ass to me. When, in truth, she was my everything.

"I need you to do something for me tomorrow. I need you to move back in with Dante."

"What?" She shifted and stared wide eyed at me.

"My life…it's fucked up right now."

She moved away from me. "So you are in trouble?"

"It's not me I'm worried about."

"Maze, what's going on? I need the truth."

I raked my hand through my hair. I'd been growing it out so it was a little longer than I normally wore it. I kept it short because I fought and didn't need to worry about anyone tugging on it in a fight. But I wasn't fighting anymore and I knew Ivy loved to run her fingers through it. "There's a war going on and I don't want you anywhere around it."

"You shouldn't be either. Let's just leave the area. We can go together. Get away until whatever is going on is over."

I raised my hand and touched the side of her face. "It's not that easy."

It wasn't. I had a lot of people depending on me now. Their businesses and livelihoods rested on my shoulders. Damn Joe. I had no idea who he truly was. Not just the financial part of it but how much he protected these people. I was too young for this shit but there was no one else and I had no choice but to learn.

Ivy shook her head. "Yes, it is. I don't want you involved. I want you safe. So if I go you go, cause I'm not going without you."

I stood and moved over to the window. Staring outside but not really seeing anything. "Babe, you really don't have much of a choice. It's for the best."

"How long?" Her voice wobbled. "How long until this is over? When you're dead?"

I swung back around when I heard the fear and tears in her voice. I moved back to the couch and knelt at her feet. I laid my hands on her thighs. "I will do everything in my power to protect you. And the only way I know how is to get you out of here. To put some distance between us."

I grabbed her waist and squeezed then looked up into her tear filled eyes. "You have got to go. After dinner I'm going to have Will take you to Dante's."

She shook her head. Her entire body trembled under my palms and I watched tears coarse down her beautiful face.

"Please, baby, no. Don't send me away I need to be with you. I won't go," she sobbed.

I got up and moved away from her. I had to move away from her. I had to do this. Her tears were destroying me. I hated the fact I was the cause but I had to stand strong. Her life depended on it. "You'll be safe with Dante. They already think we're no longer together so you'll be fine. And if they see you come into the gym with Dante it will keep you safe."

"What? Maze? NO! What do you mean we're no longer together?"

The phone on the coffee table vibrated. I went over and picked it up. There was a text from Will. The food delivery guy was on his way up. I put the phone in my pocket and rubbed my hand over my face. I knew this had to be done but goddamnit it hurt. "Yes, Ivy. For now. You have no choice." I didn't raise my voice, but I kept it cold and even. "I want you out of here and I will fucking tie you up and deliver you to Dante that way if I have to. Now call him and let him know you're moving back in."

I inwardly winced at the harshness of my tone. I heard her sharp intake of breath and knew I broke her heart but I had to. There was a knock on the door. I couldn't look at Ivy. Couldn't see her tears anymore. She would break me down if I let her. I took a moment to find my balance to get control of my emotions. There was another knock and this time I moved to answer it. I had an account at most of the local restaurants so the meals were just charged to my credit card but the delivery guys I always tipped cash.

I opened the door and reached for my wallet in my back pocket. The guy had the bag of food held high so it was in my face. Some sixth sense, if you will, or whatever the fuck had helped me win all those years in the arena kicked in. My gaze didn't drift toward the bag in my face; instead I looked down toward the delivery guy's other hand. He held black metal. His hand was already rising when I lashed out. I finished pulling out my wallet and slammed the edge right into the soft spot at his throat. I used my other hand to grab his wrist, placing pressure on a nerve to get him to drop the gun. When it fell to the floor, I released him and he crumpled to the ground.

I pulled out my phone and called Will. "Get the fuck up here now!"

"Maze!"

I quickly glanced over my shoulder at Ivy. Her eyes were wide, and her mouth was open in horror. "Babe, go in the bedroom and lock the door. Then go into the closet. Under my dresser in there, on the bottom of it, there's a gun. Get it. If anyone but me comes through that door you fucking pull the trigger."

She stood up. I could see her body shaking from where I was. "Maze."

I couldn't go to her. Couldn't comfort her just then. "Babe, please. Do it now!"

I know I yelled at her but I needed her to get out of there. I needed her safe. Cause this piece of shit was dead from that blow to his neck and if he wasn't he would be soon enough. I heard the sound of her crutch as she made her way to the bedroom and the door close. The pounding footfalls of my security echoed up the stairs as Will and Mark came tearing up them with guns drawn.

I bent down and checked the guy's pulse. Nothing. I moved the bag of food aside that had dropped to the ground and checked his pockets. I found his wallet and a cell phone. I handed both to Will.

"What happened?" Will asked.

"You fucking tell me." I got right up into Will's face. I was pissed and scared shitless. Ivy could have been killed. "You let him up here."

"I'm sorry, man. I knew you ordered food and he was here from the restaurant."

"Well fucker tried to kill me." I told Will exactly what had happened.

"Okay. We'll take care of this. Here's how we're going to handle it," Will said.

Before he could say anything I said, "Ivy was here, man. She saw it all and she's terrified."

"Can you trust her?"

I glanced in the direction of the closed door. I trusted her with my life. But she shouldn't have to put up with this. Fuck, she shouldn't have to be a part of this world. "Don't worry about her. What do you want to do?"

"First, we find out if he really works for the restaurant." Will went through the guy's wallet and found a pay stub. "Well, it looks like he does." He put it back in the wallet and placed it in the dude's pocket. He turned on the guy's phone but it was locked. The good news was it was one of those phones with thumbprint activation. He pressed the guy's thumb on it and it unlocked.

"Bingo!" Will exclaimed. He pulled out his own phone and took pictures of the last incoming and outgoing calls. "Now, here's how we're going to play this. I'll run a check on these calls. But you cannot be involved. Go back inside. Wait a half hour and call the restaurant. Ask them about the status of your food. Tell them you never got it. Go back inside and forget everything else."

Mark picked up the bag of food.

"Fuck. What are you going to do with him?" I asked.

"Best you don't know," Will replied.

"Fucking, hell." I pushed my hand through my hair. This shit was crazy. "Okay. But one more thing. I want Ivy out of here, now."

"Let us take care of this first. We just need to get him out of here. Then I'll come back in about fifteen and take her. Where am I taking her?"

I gave him the address then shut the door. I leaned against it for a minute to get my breathing under control. Trying to get my thoughts together. Oh God, she could have been killed. I knew she abhorred violence. She'd told me once about overhearing her parents talking about how her biological father almost beat her mother to death while she was pregnant with her. Her stepfather actually saved her mom. It was only now I remembered Phil was her stepdad. I ran to the bedroom door but stopped before I pulled it open. "Ivy, baby, it's me."

She opened the door and fell into my arms sobbing. She circled her arms around me and held me like she didn't want to let go. I didn't want her too nor did I want to let her leave. But we had little options before and absolutely none now. What happened proved that. I lowered my arms and grabbed her hands holding them in mine. "It's okay, baby. Everything is fine."

"Maze, that man…he…he had a gun."

"I know."

"Are the police on the way?" she sobbed.

I shook my head. "No. Will's taking care of it. The man's gone. He won't bother us again." I walked past her and saw the gun on the bed. I ignored it and grabbed the bags I'd put in there earlier. The minute I picked them up she seemed to find her voice.

"Maze, what's going on? I don't understand. What do you mean Will's taking care of it? What happened to that guy? Is he going to be okay?"

I came over to her and looked into her eyes. "I need you to listen to me very carefully. That man tried to kill me. Maybe you, too. I don't know for sure, but I've put you in danger. I swear I will not put you in the middle of this shit any more. Forget about that guy. Forget about seeing him tonight. Forget about everything that happened here tonight. In fact, you were not here."

"Maze."

Her lips turned down at the corner and her entire body trembled. I dropped the bags and just held her while she cried on my shoulder. All she did was say my name. "Shhh, babe, I know. It's going to be all right. I promise. You will be fine. I will not put you in danger again. I'm sending you to Dante. No argument."

I stepped back and wiped the tears off her face but more fell on my hand. Burning straight through me. "Damnit, baby, please. You have to go. You know you do."

The look on her face damned near dropped me to my knees. I wanted to bawl like I haven't since I was five years old and my mother died. Even more recently when Joe was killed. That's what sending Ivy away felt like. Like I'd killed a part of Ivy and me. And that shit hurt like a bitch.

"Call...call Dante." I could barely choke the words out past my pain. "Now. Do it now."

"My phone is in my purse on the coffee table."

"Okay." We moved out to the living room just as there was a knock on the door. At the same time my phone buzzed. I glanced at the phone, and saw a text from Mark letting me know Will was on the way up. I moved over to the door and checked the peephole. After seeing Will on the other side I opened the door. I handed him the bags. "We'll be down in five."

He took the bags and walked back down the hall. I turned around to see Ivy on the phone and I heard her say, "Dante...I...I need to take you up on your offer."

What fucking offer was that? I supposed I had no right to ask.

"I'll be there in fifteen." Then she hung up the phone and looked at me. Hurt, fear, love all shone in her gaze. "Okay," her voice wobbled.

I had to be strong for us both. I went to her and took her hand, and we walked out of our apartment. I didn't know if we'd ever be together there again. Mark led the way down the stairs. He opened the entrance to the street level but paused, checking the area before letting us exit the building. He walked us to the limo parked right in front and opened the door. After we got in, Mark closed the door and put the suitcases in the trunk. He got into the front passenger seat.

Will was already behind the wheel and we took off. I set the privacy glass and sat back taking Ivy's hand. She wouldn't look at me. She stared out the window but at least she didn't pull away from me. I don't think I could have taken that.

"How long?" Her voice was soft and hoarse from crying but I heard her question and understood it.

"I don't know. Until you're safe."

"And I'll be safe if I'm not with you?" she whispered.

"Yes."

"But what about you?" She turned in the seat to face me. "I can't lose you, Maze."

"I can't lose you either and that's why this has to be done."

"I'm supposed to go to the doctor tomorrow to have my cast removed. You're …you're supposed to help me with my ankle."

God she was killing me. "And I will. I promised you. If the doctor says you can begin therapy on it then we'll start work on it next week. But I only want you coming to the gym with Dante. Do you understand? Only with Dante. And you and I... You and I will be casual with each other."

The look of shock on her face at my statement was worse than when she'd seen me kill the delivery guy. "What? What are you saying, Maze? Just fucking tell me straight out."

My Ivy cussing was just all wrong. I wanted to take her in my arms and tell Will to turn around and take us back home. But I didn't, I couldn't. I let the ice invade my veins. "They have to believe we don't mean anything to each other, Ivy. There can be no us for a while. Your life depends on it."

Chapter Thirteen

Ivy

It all happened so incredibly fast. It took my mind a minute to catch up to what my eyes had seen. I was never more scared in my life and didn't know how to process it all. The only thing I understood was Maze was sending me away. With every turn of the wheel the car took me farther from the home Maze and I had created for each other. I knew there was something going on that he was somehow involved with the Triad. I should be glad to leave. To know he wanted to keep me out of it and safe. Instead, terror for him and a deep sadness invaded my soul. He could have died tonight. He still could. I turned back around to look at him.

"What do I tell Dante?"

"Don't tell him about what happened tonight. It's safer for him that way. Just tell him we had a fight. That you can't trust me, and you left me."

I shook my head. "No. No."

He took both my hands in his. "Yes, babe. You must.

It's true. I can't be trusted right now to keep you safe."

The tears didn't want to stop falling. My emotions were going haywire. "When will I see you again?"

"I don't know. Maybe next week, but call me after you talk to the doctor tomorrow."

The car pulled up in front of the building and the doorman recognized me and opened the door for us. Maze walked me inside holding my bags. Mark came behind us but left us at the entrance. We took the elevator up to Dante's floor. "I'll send the rest of your stuff over tomorrow," Maze said.

His words were like a knife through me. I still wasn't sure what was going on. Only somehow I was moving out. He was throwing me out. "No."

"I have to. You have got to go. I've made too many mistakes."

"Am I a mistake?" I sobbed. "Are we a mistake?"

"Shit. Never think that. This is on me."

The elevator halted and we stepped off. I turned and led the way down the hall and stopped in front of Dante's door. Maze knocked on it. Dante opened the door and the look of worry on his face cracked my already brittle façade. I threw myself into his arms and bawled.

"Fuck."

I heard Maze say.

"What the fuck, man?" Dante growled. "Ivy, are you all right?"

But I couldn't answer him. My heart was breaking.

"She's fine," Maze answered as he placed the bags inside the door and turned to leave.

I swung around. "Maze."

Air pressed in and out of my lungs as I waited for him to say something, anything. To hold me, take me into his arms and tell me everything would be all right. He'd take me home and we'd be together forever. But it wasn't happening. I watched him freeze. For a moment I thought he'd reconsider and realize we had to be together. We needed each other. I couldn't lose him. But he didn't.

Instead, without turning around to face me, he replied, "It's for the best, babe."

I watched him put one foot in front of the other and walk away from me. Dante closed the door, and if he hadn't been holding me up, I would have crumbled to the floor. He carried me over to the couch and sat down with me, holding me close against his side.

"I'm sorry, hon. So sorry. What happened?"

I shook my head. "Please. I can't talk about this right now. Tomorrow, okay? We'll talk tomorrow."

"Just tell me are you all right. He didn't hurt you or anything?"

I snorted. How do I answer that? Yes, he hurt me. He ripped out my heart but not the way Dante meant. "No. He didn't hurt me. Not that way."

I pulled away from Dante. "Thank you for taking me in. I'm sorry if I upset any plans you had tonight, but please don't worry about me. I'll be fine." I grabbed my crutch and stood. Dante did as well.

"Don't you worry about it. I had no plans for tonight and even if I did you'd come first. Here let me get your bags and take them to your room. I haven't touched a thing in there."

"What would I do without you?" I asked. I put one arm around his waist and hugged him before stepping away and going to my old bedroom. He placed my things on the floor by the bed and I sat down on the comforter. I'd left all of my sheets behind.

"You'll never have to find out," he replied in answer to my question. "Are you hungry? I ordered a pizza earlier and there's some left."

"No. I just want to go to sleep. I've got to get up in the morning and go to the doctor tomorrow." I spoke the truth. I was no longer hungry. It had been sucked right out of me.

"Oh, that's right. You get the cast off tomorrow. What

time?"

"Nine-thirty."

"Okay, I'll go with you."

"You don't have to do that, Dante. I can take a cab."

He moved his head from side to side. "I want to. We're partners as well as best friends. I'm always there for you."

He bent down and kissed my forehead then before I could say thank you he closed my door behind him as he left. I pulled myself up on the bed until I could stretch the full length on it. The tears came again. For a while I feared they wouldn't stop. I still didn't know what had happened tonight, but I did know Maze was in danger and I couldn't be with him. He didn't even give me the option. He didn't want me with him. I curled up into a ball and cried some more. The chime on my phone had me sitting up, rushing for the purse I'd dropped on the floor beside the crutch. It was a text from Maze. Three words but they meant everything. He was everything.

Maze: *I love you.*

I texted him back I loved him too, begging him to come and get me.

When nothing else came through I knew he was gone.

I cried myself to sleep that night. And I still wasn't sure why he had to send me away and pretend we weren't together. I could never pretend I didn't want him. Love him.

I got up early the next morning in the clothes I'd fallen asleep in. My head hurt, my eyes were puffy, and my heart still felt like it had shattered into a hundred pieces.

Maze... How could he send me away?

I got off the bed and opened my suitcase, taking out a change of clothes. It's a good thing I still had a few clean things in there. When Dante and I were in Philly, we stayed with his aunt and uncle, and his aunt washed clothes for me.

I went into the bathroom and brushed my teeth. I opted for a long hot shower. It took awhile because I had two crying fits in there. Finally, I finished washing up and got dressed. I found my way into the kitchen and made myself a bowl of oatmeal.

Sitting at the table, I tasted nothing I placed into my mouth. I might as well have been eating air. I choked down another spoon full of the oatmeal and made sure I finished the bowl. I hadn't eaten since lunch yesterday and I needed to eat. So I forced it.

My thoughts focused on Maze and what had happened last night. Why I found myself back where I'd begun so many months ago without Maze. Well, not quite. Even a couple of weeks ago, dance was everything to me. Being able to dance again was at the forefront of my thoughts. The goal I set for myself and facing an alternative if I couldn't. But suddenly, none of it mattered. The most important thing in my life was missing. Maze alive and well took prominence in my thoughts.

Dante came out of his room stark naked. As soon as he saw me he froze. "Sorry," he said. "I forgot."

"Don't mind me." I smiled.

He really had nothing to be sorry for. I'd forgotten he liked to walk around in the buff and had only curbed it after we started living together. I see he went back to old habits. He was slender yet muscled like Maze, but his thighs were a little bigger and his chest a bit wider. Typical of male dancers who had to do a lot of lifts. They needed that little extra touch of strength. Yet I had no doubt Maze could lift me with ease.

I was sorry to put Dante out again but relieved when he turned around and went back into his room. It didn't escape my notice his dick twitched as he watched me watching him. Maybe it wasn't such a good idea my being here. I knew how Dante really felt about me. But he also knew how I felt about Maze. Maze. All roads led me back to him.

I heard the shower in Dante's room go on and I cleaned up the small mess I'd made in the kitchen. Then I went back to my room to unpack my stuff and put them away. The few clothes that were still dirty I left on the floor to wash later. I remembered Maze saying he'd have the rest of my things sent over today. The thought brought another pang to my already arching heart. I grabbed my purse and by the time I'd returned to the kitchen Dante was seated at the table eating his bowl of cereal.

He pushed the chair across from him out. "Sit. Talk," he said.

Reluctantly, I sat down. Knowing I wasn't going to get out of this but at the same time not sure what I should say. Maze already told me I couldn't tell him the truth. And while I didn't want to lie to Dante, I would not betray Maze. But I owed Dante an explanation. I frowned as a thought occurred to me. Dante owed me an explanation, too. "I know you're not gay and you're not bi either."

He grinned sheepishly.

"Why lie to me?"

"I didn't exactly lie. I just let you continue to think a certain way. I wanted you…to live with me. I liked you, but I knew you'd never go for it if you really knew how much."

I sighed. "I'm sorry…"

He shook his head. "No, apologies. You never lied to me or made me any promises. I always knew where your heart lay. Even before Maze came back into your life. And after he did it was damn obvious. So please, don't be sorry. Now, tell me what happened between you and Maze."

I took his hand and held it tightly for a moment before releasing it. "We had an argument and we thought it best that I move out. At least for now while Maze figures out a few things." There I said it, like it made sense and with a straight face. While inside my heart cried.

Dante frowned. "Is he fighting again?"

Dante knew damn well how I felt about that. He was also aware Maze had retired. "No. That's not it exactly. He's only training fighters."

"So he's still involved with the Triad. Is that what this is about?"

Damn, I didn't want Dante going down that road. "I don't know but I don't want him in the ring, cage, arena whatever, again. He'd promised me but he's signed on a couple of new fighters." All of those things are true.

"Wow, Ivy. You left the guy over that?"

"Stupid, huh?" The uncertainty in my voice bled through.

He leaned forward and gave me a hug. "No. Not at all. I'm not going to quibble over getting my best friend and roommate back."

"This is only temporary, Dante. Maze and I just need a

little time apart." At least that's what I needed to keep telling myself.

Dante held up his hands. "You take all the time you need." He glanced over my shoulder. "I told my limo service to pick us up out front in five minutes, so if you're ready we can head downstairs now."

"I'm ready."

****

Dante didn't need to help me back into the limo. No more crutch or cast. Well not like I had before. I now had a walking cast or boot, and permission to do some light exercises for my ankle. The nurse had given me a sheet of exercises I should begin doing and a list of things I should not do. I had to wear the walking cast anytime I left the house, and even at home I had to keep pressure off my ankle as much as possible. Baby steps. As we sat in the car, I texted Maze my news but I got no reply from him.

"Well, at least you're cleared for some exercise. We can go to the gym…"

I assumed he meant our regular gym, but that's not where I wanted to go. "Okay. We'll go to Maze's gym next week." He promised me and I intended to hold him to his promise of helping me.

"What? Are you sure?"

"Yes. He put aside a room for us. He's got it all set up like a mini ballet studio. Complete with wood floors for pointe, a ballet bar, and mirrors." Just the thought of those mirrors caused my stomach muscles to clench in memory of how we christened that room.

"No, shit?"

I grinned. "Yeah. I'll let him know when to expect us next week. I'll give him the sheets the nurse gave me so he'll know what not to do."

Dante shook his head. "Are you sure about this, Ivy? Being around him like that?"

Something told me going to the gym was the only way he'd let me near him. And as pathetic as it might be, if that was the only way to get near Maze, then that's the way it had to be.

"Yes. I'll be fine."

Chapter Fourteen

Maze

The base of my neck tingled. I glanced over at the front doors and my gaze locked onto Ivy.

"Run through that set two more times," I said to the young fighter I'd been working with. I made a straight line to Ivy and Dante. They hadn't moved from near the entrance. I didn't stop until I stood in front of them. It had been more than a week since I'd seen her. All I wanted to do was pull her into my arms and then take her upstairs and make love to her until neither one of us could walk. But it wasn't going to happen. Too many eyes were on us. I didn't know how much longer this stalemate between the Tong and the Triad would last. Tsang found out the Triad sent the assassin and he was doing all he could to extract us, but it would take time. Meanwhile, we wait. As long as the Triad thought they couldn't hurt me or get to me we remained in limbo. All I cared about was clearing Ivy off their radar. I made it a point to greet Dante and not touch Ivy. I saw her body leaning toward me, already expecting and anticipating my touch. *Fuck...*

"Hey, man," I said to Dante, holding out my hand to shake his. We grasped hands in greeting. He grabbed mine a little on the tight side.

Dante's gazed at me with narrowed eyes, making it clear he wasn't sure if they should be there. He said, "Thanks for letting us use your place."

I smiled trying to put him and myself at ease. "Hey, no worries. It's already set up for you."

I led them to the room I had designed for Ivy and opened the door, moving farther into the space. The first thing I saw was the image of Ivy in the mirror and memories hit me like a freight train. Ivy under me, me inside her, our bodies merged, blending, no beginning and no ending as we made love on the mat, on the floor, against the ballet bar. My gaze snapped to hers and I saw her watching me in the mirror. I knew her thoughts reflected mine. She seemed to freeze in the doorway. Dante stood next to her and placed his hand on her back, giving her a little push forward. She stepped across the threshold and came in, Dante behind her.

"Close the door, will ya, man?" I requested. My voice took on a cadence I didn't recognize. One of sadness.

As soon as he did I took three steps to reach Ivy and pulled her into my arms. I couldn't stand it anymore. My mouth covered hers, our bodies curled into each other and she clung to me. Finally, at last, my heart beat, my blood flowed. I could breathe again.

"I've missed you," I whispered moving my lips to her ear, her neck.

I had my hands on her ass and picked her up. She wrapped her legs around my waist in response. I wanted to strip her, put her on the floor, and be buried inside her in seconds. I was moments away from my heaven when the sound of a loud cough caught my attention.

"FUCK!" I roared.

"Do you two need to be alone?" Dante asked.

"No," I growled. Putting Ivy down, I stepped back. I took a couple of deep breaths to get my shit together.

Ivy continued to stare at me, a mixture of lust and deep sadness in her gaze. I couldn't stare at her for long I'd take her back into my arms. Not sure I'd be able to let her go again if I did.

Dante glanced back and forth between us. "So everything cool between you two now?"

"No," I said, not glancing at either one of them but I felt Ivy's gaze boring into me, willing me to look at her. I did and saw the misery tearing in her eyes. Misery I also felt. I shook my head. "No. Let's just do this."

She didn't say a word, just wiped her hand over her eyes.

I pulled out the mats I kept in there for their use and gave them each one. They stripped down to their workout gear and Ivy took off the new walking boot. She handed me the sheet the nurse had given her and I scanned it. "This is fine. The stuff I have in mind for you for the next couple of weeks should be okay. I'll go over the exercises with you now but some of them you'll be able to do at home and Dante can help you. So, Dante, I need you to pay attention to what I'm doing."

After they both nodded, I spent the next forty minutes showing them some exercises. Then I spent more time watching both Ivy and Dante repeat what they'd learned. Once I was satisfied, I left them to work on their own. I spent the next hour doing everything but going anywhere near the door to the ballet room. Yet, the minute the door opened and Ivy walked out into the main area, I knew it. Even though I was on the other side of the room. Dante saw me and waved. I waved back but stayed right where I was. By sheer force of will, I kept myself from crossing the room. Refusing to respond to the pull of Ivy's silent plea. Oh, she was calling me. I could hear her as clear as day even if no one else could. After what felt like forever, she and Dante moved toward the exit. I continued to stand there, holding the punching bag and aching in every part of my soul.

For the last few days, I stayed at the gym until late. I'd see Ivy and Dante come in and then leave. I'd spend twenty minutes with them and leave them alone. I didn't even really need to do that, but I needed to touch her if only for a minute while I worked her ankle. I was slowly going crazy.

After they left this evening, I got into the center ring and took on anyone who wanted to fight. At the end of the night, I was the last man standing. Even though drenched in sweat, and my body ached, nothing dulled the pain of knowing I'd go up those stairs to my apartment and Ivy won't be there.

I closed up the place and took the elevator from the gym up to the apartment to take a shower. Tonight instead of passing out from exhaustion, as I'd done other nights, I was wired. I couldn't relax, couldn't sleep. I'd gotten a text earlier from Vin to hang out with him again. I'd done it a couple of times when Ivy was in Philly. But this time, I really just needed to get out of the apartment. I was too alone here. I missed Ivy so much, and I feared I'd cave in and go get her if I stayed. I texted Will and he brought the car around and we headed downtown.

The club was packed but most people were on the dance floor. I headed straight for the bar and found a seat at the very end. I pulled out my phone and texted Vin I was there, sitting at the end of the bar. When the bar maid came over to my end I flagged her and placed an order.

"And when you see that one low don't bother to wait to ask I want a refill," I said.

She nodded. I glanced around to see if I saw any familiar faces, I didn't. But everything was a blur really. I was only there because I figured it was better to be alone in a crowded room than in an empty apartment. A strong odor of citrus and clover assailed my senses before I felt her touch on my shoulder. The bartender laid my drink on the counter in front of me at the same time the woman behind me came around to stand at my side. I didn't bother to even glance at her. I just reached for my drink.

"What's that?" she asked, a sexy breathiness to her voice.

"My drink," I said, and took a gulp.

"Wanna buy me one?"

"No."

"Bastard!"

I didn't bother to respond. I finished my first drink and was lifting the second when Vin finally showed up.

"Hey, man," he said, grabbing my shoulders. "Looks like you started this party without me." He glanced over at the bar maid and got her attention. "I'll have the same thing."

I stood so he wasn't standing over me, and besides, I was tired of sitting.

Once he got his drink, we moved over to one of the high tables that became available and placed our drinks on it. It was a better position to check out the crowd. Not that I really paid much attention to anything, but Vin was. He kept commenting on the women checking us out. I couldn't even pretend interest. No surprise when two of them approached us. Vin made them feel welcome. I didn't give a fuck.

He bought them both drinks. He carried on most of the conversation, and I only grunted. I finished my forth drink and still felt as miserable as I did before I left the house. Before the redhead could drag my friend off to the dance floor I tapped his arm.

"I'm gonna bounce, man."

"No, don't go. Fuck, man, it's barely eleven." He turned to grin at the blonde who'd been trying to get my attention all night. "At least if you go you don't have to go alone." He grinned.

I didn't even bother to glance in the woman's direction

he kept staring at.

"Laters." I fist bumped him and made my way through the horde toward the exit. I pulled out my phone and texted Will. But the place was crowded and loud and I just wanted out. When I got outside, I texted him to meet me at the corner. I walked out into the warm evening air and it cleared my head a little. I turned and headed in the direction where I told Will to pick me up. It wasn't all that late, but this was New York, the city that never sleeps, and it was more than making up for that rep. I leaned against the building at the cross street but I didn't have long to wait before Will pulled up on the road.

I pushed myself off the wall and approached the car, not giving Will a chance to get out and open the door for me. I opened it myself and got in. "Take me home."

I lay my head back against the soft leather and shut my eyes, trying to clear my thoughts when my phone rang. I checked the phone and saw it was Dante. Ivy had put his number in my phone before they'd taken their trip.

I answered. "Hey, man, what's up? Everything okay?"

"Maze."

Something in his voice sent a chill down my spine.

"Is Ivy with you?" Dante asked.

"Fuck, no. What the hell is going on?"

"Oh, Jesus. Don't panic. I dropped her off at the theatre earlier tonight. She wanted to stop in and talk to Davis, one of the director's of the company who was working late. She told me she'd catch a cab home. There are always cars in the area so I knew it wouldn't be a problem. We were supposed to go to dinner."

I pulled the phone away to yell. "Will, head for the place we dropped Ivy off." When he nodded, I placed the phone back to my ear. "When was she supposed to be back?"

"She's running a couple hours late. I called Davis. She left over an hour ago."

The blood in my veins froze. "I'm on my way to your place. Have you tried calling her?"

"Yeah. Goes straight to voicemail. Like the phone is turned off."

"Fuck! Be there in five." I hung up.

Leaning forward I spoke to my driver again. "Will, can you hurry? Ivy's missing." I called Ivy's number, but my call got treated no differently from Dante's, straight to voicemail. I sent her a text telling her to call or text. Then I called Tsang.

"Ivy's missing."

"I'll make a few calls. I'll also have someone check to see if she's back at the gym."

"I doubt she's there. She's not answering her phone."

"I'll find her, Maze," Tsang said. "Hang tight. I'll call you back after I talk to a few folks."

"We're here."

The sound of Will's voice had me looking out the window. I didn't even realize we'd arrived at Dante's condo. I was out of the car before he'd fully pulled to a stop. The doorman opened the door for me and I moved past him and headed straight for the elevator then the condo. I only had to knock once before Dante pulled the door open. I walked in and stopped before turning to face him.

"What the fuck happened?" I yelled.

"You fucking tell me!" Dante yelled back, getting right up in my face. "I know whatever is going on has to do with whatever fucked up shit you're involved in. And whatever that is you've dragged Ivy into it."

"Shit," I said, turning aside.

It was either that or take the motherfucker down. But my anger was wasted on him. He was right. This shit was on my head. If she was missing only one person would have dared to take her. I spun around and headed for the door without a word. But Dante wasn't letting me leave that easily. He moved in front of me and grabbed my arm pulling me to a stop.

I looked him right in the eyes. "Get your fucking hand off me."

He shook his head but kept his eyes on mine. "Where are you going? We need to call the cops."

"Only if you want Ivy dead. Now get your fucking hand off me. I'm not going to tell you again."

He let go slowly, letting me know he wasn't scared of me, and I saw the message in his gaze. If he could he'd kick my ass. In truth, I couldn't blame him for thinking it.

"Do you know where she is?" he asked.

"I…I think I know who did it."

Dante raked his fingers through his locks. "Can you get her back?"

"You'll know if I fail. I'll be dead."

"Fuck, man."

I continued to head toward the door. My hand rested on the knob when his voice gave me pause.

"I'm coming with you."

I turned back. "Thanks, but for Ivy to stand a chance, I have to do this alone."

I shut the door behind me and returned to the limo.

"Take me back to the apartment, Will." There were things there I'd need if Liu held Ivy. She could be anywhere. But I knew where Liu would be or at least who could find him if he wasn't home. I called Tsang. "Where's Liu?"

"Maze, I still have people out looking for Ivy. Forget about Liu for now."

"I know. But it might already be too late. Is Liu at his home?"

"Not that I know of, why?"

"Because we both know the son of a bitch took her."

"Even if he did, he's not stupid enough to keep her at his home. Let me find her, Maze. I swear to you I will. Don't do anything stupid."

"Thank you, Uncle Tsang."

"I've sent people out to the places Liu owns."

"Good."

"And, Maze, stay away from Liu. His place is going to be crawling with his security. Wait for my call."

"I know, but..."

"You know she's not at his house. Let me handle this."

"I know."

"Don't worry, Maze, we'll find her."

I hung up the phone after that. I knew what he was thinking. Find Ivy first then go after Liu. We'd find her one way or another. But in the depths of my soul I knew she was alive. And I could see only one way out of all of this.

Chapter Fifteen

Ivy

The walking cast made it so much easier to move around. And I felt really good after my meeting with Davis. As long as I was ready for the fall performance I'd still be their featured artist, and he knew about the piece Dante and I choreographed for his old dance studio. Davis was very supportive and seemed sure it would be chosen for the festival. In fact, he planned on flying down for the performance nights, and he wanted Dante and me to create a special featured piece. My future loomed brighter, at least my professional future. I'd come to terms with the time I wouldn't be able to dance. And I had Maze to thank for that. Maze. I hurt just thinking about us. I saw him almost every day at the gym, so close and yet so far. Since that first time Dante and I went there and he'd shut the door and taken me into his arms, I thought everything would be fine. He'd let me move back in. We'd be together again, but he hadn't touched me that way since then. The only thing he did was work with me by doing the exercises together. Even though his touch was professional it still sent jolts through me. It was both frustrating and fun to work with him. My ankle felt better but I still had a long way to go before I could even attempt to put on pointe shoes.

I walked outside to a pleasant evening, enjoying the fact most of the theatres weren't out yet, so not much foot traffic. I moved toward the edge of the sidewalk to flag down the next cab. One pulled over almost immediately. Another car drew up behind it. I didn't pay much attention to it. I stepped off the sidewalk, and had my hand on the door handle of the cab. Suddenly, someone grabbed me around my waist from behind. Literally picked me up, then walked a few steps and threw me face first in the backseat of the car stopped behind the cab.

I tried to turn over and kick out, to push the person back who got into the car behind me, but he shifted and punched me in the face, snapping my face to the side.

The pain rattled through my brain. Momentarily stunning me. He used the opportunity to twist me back onto my stomach, grab my legs, and sit on them immobilizing me. My cheek where his fist connected stung. I must have bitten my lip because I tasted the metallic tang of blood on my tongue. My breaths came in gulps and I fought not to cry.

The car lurched forward and stopped abruptly. I rolled onto the floor into an awkward position. We continued driving again. Fast. I had to get out of there. But I feared I wouldn't be able to. Still I had to fight. I pushed myself up, trying to sit up and get back on the seat. Strong hands grabbed me around the waist and hauled be back on the seat.

"Get the hell off me!" I screamed.

"Shut the fuck up, bitch." He managed to hold me face down.

He yanked my hair hard and raised my chin off the seat. I thought he might have pulled out a few strands. I caught a glimpse of a blue denim sleeve before he wrapped a bandanna or something over my eyes, then he tied my hands behind my back. I managed to flip onto my side and tried to kick him with the boot, but he pushed my legs down, turned me on my stomach again, and placed his hand on the flat of my back. He sat against my thighs, using his bulk to keep me pinned down.

Terror infused my veins, giving me strength but no matter how much I bucked against him I couldn't budge him off me. Breathing hard, I quieted. I gave my brain a chance to run through possible solutions, but came up empty. Maze had been right to want to keep me away from any violence, but he'd been wrong, too. He should never have sent me away. But I knew he would find me. I just had to hold on until he did.

I love you, Maze.

I just hoped he wouldn't be too late.

The captor in the back with me began to cup my ass and feel between my legs. I whimpered, and when he tried to pull my yoga pants down I shifted and tried to fight him in earnest. Sharp words spoken by the driver had them yelling at each other but at least he stopped. They spoke what sounded like Chinese to me. When I'd been pushed into the car everything happened quickly, but I thought the driver at least was Chinese. They had to be Triad.

I don't know how long we drove. I lost track of time. Eventually, we came to a stop and I heard the front passenger's side door open. Then the door near my head opened. Someone grabbed my shoulders and pulled me out of the car. As soon as my feet hit the graveled ground, I stumbled but rough hands held me steady. One muscular arm wrapped around my waist. The other held onto my arm and forced me to walk forward.

I walked. I had no choice. I went up two steps and then the ground changed. It felt like I walked on a carpeted floor. Then I took a few steps before I was turned, walked some more then pushed. I would have fallen if I didn't find my balance. I wasn't a ballerina for nothing. Whoever came in behind me grabbed my arm, pulling me, and then shoved my shoulder against what felt like a wall. He pushed me down until I landed on the floor.

I scooted backward, away from him. I kept the wall against me until I backed into a corner. I remained blindfolded, my hands still tied behind my back. Really, where was I going? My captors knew that would be nowhere, so I stopped and tried to calm myself. I stuck my legs straight out and rested my head against the wall. I thought perhaps I was in an empty room with only my assailants for company.

I heard someone else enter the room and he spoke to whoever stood over me in Chinese. Suddenly, the bandanna was yanked from around my eyes. I blinked to adjust to the dim light and tried to get my bearings. The first thing I noticed was there were two men in the room, and another who remained near the door, but he didn't come into the room. All of the men seemed about the same height. Two were slender, and one appeared a little overweight. They all wore black hooded sweatshirts, the hoods drawn up over their heads. Only one wore a blue denim jacket over the sweatshirt. The same one who'd been in the backseat with me. They also wore bandannas that covered them from the nose down. All I could see were the slants of their dark eyes. Triad. I stifled the cry of fear threatening to emerge.

"Who…who are you? Why am I here?" Didn't come out as strong as I wanted.

The one at the door said something to the others. They stared at me then turned and left the room. The slightly pudgy guy at the door remained behind.

"Do you need to use the bathroom?" he asked.

His voice was heavily accented, but I don't know if it was because that's the way he spoke or if he did it on purpose. I thought perhaps the latter to cover the sound of his voice. I started to say no, but decided to ask a question instead. Not that my first couple were answered. "Do you plan on keeping me here long?"

"Do you need to use the bathroom or not?"

"Yes."

He came over to me and placed the bandanna that had been dropped to the floor back around my eyes.

I whimpered. "Please, don't do that. I can't identify you."

Again, he ignored me. He merely helped me stand and led me out of the room. We took a left and seemed to head in a different direction from the way we entered. After a few steps we went down another set of stairs, then we came to a stop. I heard a door open and he shoved me through it. He pulled the bandanna off and untied the binding around my wrists.

As soon as my hands were released, I pulled them in front of me and massaged them. The restraints weren't really tight but having my hands tied like that was not comfortable. I glanced around. I seemed to be in some sort of commercial establishment. This was not the kind of bathroom you'd find in someone's home. It wasn't that big, wide enough for a toilet, a sink, and a paper towel dispenser and trashcan. Not a window in sight.

"You have five minutes." Then the man left.

I'd been hoping there'd be a window, something I could use in there, but unlike the movies there was nothing. No way out or to signal for help. They'd taken my purse with my cell phone in it. I looked at my face in the mirror. I saw my cheek was already turning a nice shade of purple. At least my lip from where I bit it no longer bled. With nothing else to do, I took advantage of the bathroom. When I finished, I washed my hands. My captor must have been standing on the other side of the door listening for the water, because he opened the door just as I reached for something to dry my hands with. He waited for me to finish.

"Turn around and put your hands behind your back."

"Please," I said. "That's not very comfortable. Especially if I'm going to be tied up for awhile."

"Hold your hands out in front then."

I did and he replaced the restraints then retied the bandanna. We repeated in reverse the way we'd come. Once we got back to the room, he removed the eye covering and I took a spot against the wall of the empty place. There was nothing in there but four walls, an air vent above my head, and a low wattage light bulb in the center of the ceiling. The door was the only way in or out. At least I wouldn't be kept alone in a dark room. "How long do you plan on keeping me here?"

"That depends. I suggest you sit down and wait." Then he turned around and walked out the door, shutting it behind him.

I waited a few minutes to make sure he'd left before going over to the door. I put my ear against the center of it but couldn't hear anything on the other side. I took a deep breath and grabbed the handle. I turned the knob and tried to push and then pull, but it was locked.

Sighing in resignation, I moved away from the door and sat down, my back once again to the wall. I stretched my legs straight out and did the only thing I could do. I waited. Knowing in my heart, I was merely bait for Maze. On the one hand, I knew he'd come for me. On the other, I hoped he wouldn't. I saw the guns all three men carried. While Maze might dodge or deflect a blow or even a sword he couldn't out maneuver a bullet.

I must have dozed because the next thing I became aware of was the feel of someone squeezing my breast. I opened my mouth to a live nightmare and screamed.

The man kneeling beside me slapped me across the face. I tried to scramble away. He grabbed for my foot but I raised my encased foot and kicked him in the face. I struggled to get to my feet, but he grabbed my arm and got me back down on the ground.

"Bitch!" he roared, blood dripping from his nose. His bandanna had fallen off and I saw his face. He fell on top of me, holding me down. Suffocating me. I screamed. He put his hand over my mouth and then suddenly his weight lifted off me.

I raised my head. The one in a black hoodie with black jeans that had taken me to the bathroom, stood in the room and spoke sharply to my attacker. Asshole turned to look at me, wiped the blood from his nose with his sleeve and grinned before walking out of the room. My savoir glanced back at me. I curled myself up into a ball on the ground and turned away from him.

I felt him kneel behind me and when he touched my arm I flinched. "Please. Leave me alone. Let me go."

"It will be over soon."

"Fuck you," I said.

"He will not bother you again."

Then he left the room and all I could do was shut my eyes and think of Maze.

Chapter Sixteen

Maze

We circled the area trying to spot all the guards surrounding the house. Will stopped around the block. "I don't like this, Maze. I don't like you going in alone."

It wasn't difficult to find out where Liu lived. I just asked Will if he knew, and he made a few calls. Dude had connections. "Will, I can do this. I've done stuff like this before and I do it best alone."

"All right. I'll give you five minutes then I'm coming in."

"Ten. And in case anyone else shows up, keep them out." I knew this was what Tsang didn't want me to do, but it had to be done.

The yards of the homes on the block were small, even if the houses appeared too big for the size of the lots. A big tree stood between the property on the left and the home I needed to break in to. I guessed which room was Liu's immediately, the corner one on the second floor. It had a balcony, and lots of windows and seemed to be the largest on this side of the house. His wife and kids were probably home. But I hoped the other rooms were well away from the larger corner room. I only wanted Liu.

I got out of the car and climbed over the brick fence of the house next door. Using the drainpipe, I made my way to the roof. There was only one way to get into Liu's house both unseen and without having to fight my way in. That would be the balcony. From Will and my count, there were two guards outside and at least two more Will and I could see moving around inside. This seemed on the looser side of security to me, but the address wasn't easy to come by. The bastard was probably over confident as to his safety.

From the roof of the house next door to Liu's, I jumped onto the upper branches of the tree. From there, it was easy to make my way to the roof of the house, bypassing the men circling the property on the ground.

I'd tried to avoid a direct confrontation with Liu but from the time he'd called a hit on Joe, I knew this was inevitable. In spite of everything I would have been willing to walk away. Let Liu keep the fucking Triad and do whatever he wanted to do with it. I told Tsang as much. I cut ties with anything Triad related. The Tong was legitimate 100%. Joe had seen to that, inevitably paying for it in his blood. But it wasn't good enough for Liu. Bastard wanted it all. The reason he had Ivy. I was not going to let that one go. I'd be spilling blood again tonight, but not my own. And God have mercy on Liu's soul if he'd hurt Ivy.

I looked over the side of the roof onto the balcony below. The night was a warm one, so I wasn't surprised to find the doors open. The curtains covering it flowed gently on the breeze.

All my senses heightened. I waited for the sentry in the front yard to move to the other side of the house. As soon as he turned to walk in the other direction, I lowered myself from the roof to the balcony. I stayed in the corner, letting the night and my dark clothing cloak me from immediate sight. I strained to listen for any sound of wakefulness from the occupants in the room. Finding none, I took my first step into the room, then another. My eyes had already adjusted to the dim lighting. I saw Liu's wife lying on the far side of the bed. I approached her first.

Taking the vial I had in my pocket, I opened it and held it under her nose. She breathed the sleeping potion in, ensuring she would continue to slumber and remain unharmed. Her husband would not be so lucky. I doubted Ivy was in the house with his wife and family but I was taking no chances.

I locked their bedroom door then made my way around the bed to Liu. I pulled my blade and placed it under the man's chin at the same time I covered his mouth.

Liu woke up with a jerk, and the knife pressed into his chin drew a sliver of blood. I watched the older man's eyes grow wide with fear. I smiled. I saw Liu's gaze dart to the side toward his wife. "She's fine and will stay that way until our business is finished. Your family is safe from me even if mine is not from you. Now get the fuck up. Slow."

I eased off so Liu could sit up. I didn't release the knife from below his chin but I moved my hand from his mouth to wrap around his bicep. I pulled him roughly to his feet.

"Is Ivy here?"

Liu's eyebrows rose in surprise, and he slowly shook his head from side to side.

I wanted a little more privacy for what I needed to do. "Bathroom," I stated.

Liu turned, leading the way. I kept pace with him until we got to a closed door. I slowly pushed it open to see a large bathroom. I pushed him over the threshold, and reached my hand on the wall to turn on the light. Then I shut the door. There was another door in the far corner of the bathroom. I shoved Liu over to it. It opened to reveal the toilet closet. Perfect for additional noise reduction and privacy. I nodded toward the small room. "Get the fuck inside."

Sweat beaded across Liu's brow. "What are you going to do?"

"Get the fuck inside. Don't make me repeat myself."

Liu went into the toilet closet. I stepped in after him and shut this door, also. Liu made the mistake of trying to clip me on the knees and make me drop the knife.

It didn't work.

I read the signs of his body as soon as he thought of the move and I blocked the blow. I delivered one of my own to the man's chest causing him to ass plant on the closed toilet seat.

In a chilling voice, I said, "Now we can do this the civilized way or not. Your choice. I'm going to ask you one question and I fucking better get the right answer the first time."

Liu ran his hand over his face. "Now you want to talk. I've been trying to get to you for awhile now, Maze."

"Yeah, I bet. Too bad I put all your boys six feet under."

Liu shook his head. "Believe it or not none of them, including Jai, acted under my orders. I know what you think. No love is lost between the two of us but it wasn't me who killed Joe. I wanted him out. Not necessarily dead."

I snorted and crossed my arms over my chest, still holding the blade in a way if he so much as twitched the wrong way he'd regret it. As he watched the knife in my hand, I thought he knew it, too.

"Bullshit." My voice was soft but Liu shivered at the one word.

"Look, my father put a hit on Joe a long time ago but he survived, and Joe and I came to an understanding."

"My mother didn't survive that fucking hit."

"Neither did my father. Which is why as far as I was concerned your family lost something and so did mine."

"Fucking ancient history, man. Let's talk current. You killed Joe, tried to kill me, and now you took Ivy. I was willing to walk away but no, you had to be greedy."

"I'm telling you I did not put out the order to kill Joe, loose cannons went after you and I did not take Ivy."

My hand with the knife flashed out fast and sliced through his shoulder. By the time Liu registered the pain I'd returned to standing in a neutral position.

"Shit," he yelled and glanced at the blood seeping through his light blue nightshirt. His hand went up to the cut.

"The next one will be deeper," I growled.

"Maze, I swear to you on the heads of my kids. I did not put the hit on Joe, or you, and I'm not the one who took

Ivy."

"Then if not you, then fucking who?"

He bowed his head, then raised it to look me in the eye. "The same person who killed my father."

That shocked the shit outta me. "What the fuck?"

"He and Joe were like brothers. But when your mother was killed Joe seemed to lose the will to lead. I took my father's place at the Triad table. It's no secret I wanted to lead. I have no love for the Tong and I did what I could to ensure the Triad controlled it. The only way to do that was to control Joe. And the Triad did until recently. There was a power play all right, but I wasn't the one behind it. I want you to think about something. How did I know the route Joe was taking from the hospital in advance enough to block the road? That took timing and pre-planning. How the fuck would me or my people know?"

I didn't like where the thoughts driven by his words were taking me. "You could have been watching the hospital and followed them the same way you've been following me."

He shook his head. "I could. But I wasn't. And even if I was how did I get far enough ahead of them to set the ambush?"

My body went rigid. The blood traveling through my

veins flowed hot. "And Ivy?"

Again he moved his head. "Why would I take her? You were out. You'd agreed to head the Tong."

"And took the money and political influence with me."

"Yes. Not lying that's a setback for us, but still what would taking Ivy get me but dead? There is only one person who benefits from my death. One person who wanted it all more than I did. One person who had his feet deeply embedded in both sides."

"No," I whispered. The fear snaking down my spine almost numbed my mind. It already numbed my soul. Each word out of his mouth confused the shit out of me. My thoughts seemed impossible. My entire life took on another meaning. Something sinister had ingrained itself in Joe's life and mine, and Joe had died as a result. Ivy was endangered as a result. "No," I spoke again. "You're lying."

He had to be.

"If I am then I'm as good as dead. I've had my people watching some of the warehouses Joe owned. I got a text earlier tonight. Check my phone. There's an address in there. If you look into it you'll see who owns that warehouse. Joe didn't own it by himself."

I'd gotten a list of all the properties Joe owned. It included a couple of warehouses, but only one had a co-owner. "Where the fuck is your phone?"

"In the bedroom on my nightstand."

"Take off your fucking shirt."

"What?"

"You heard me." After he did I tied his hands behind his back and opened the bathroom door. Holding onto his arm, I marshaled us back to his room over to the bed. He glanced at his sleeping wife.

"She'll be fine," I said. "She'll sleep till morning and wake up feeling refreshed. Provided you are truthful."

We went around the bed and his cell rested right where he said it would. I picked it up and pressed the home button. It was locked but he gave me the code. I glanced at the last message and sure enough it was an address. One over in Chelsea where I remembered one of the storage places was listed. I scrolled back through the conversation and my heart skipped a beat as I found more proof of what he said was true. From the text when he'd been alerted Ivy had been snatched, to when he'd gotten a report she'd been seen taken into the warehouse.

I put the phone back down on the nightstand and turned to look at Liu who sat on the bed. I untied his hands.

"Yeah, I've had some of Tsang's people followed. I was never your enemy, Maze. I was even willing to let Joe leave for a price. That price was you taking the fall in the fight. Which you won, costing me. But even then Joe covered my losses. He made things right."

What? I didn't know that. What the fuck was going on here? Liu kept talking. "Yes. Joe wanted out and he wanted to make sure there'd be no negative repercussions for you. Do you know he called me and I went to see him at the hospital?" Liu sighed when I didn't respond. "Yeah, didn't think so. You should have come to see me before this. It would have been almost impossible for me to try to come and see you. As far as I'm concerned the blood spilled between us is even. Stay the fuck outta my business and I'll stay away from yours."

I studied this man who had just turned my world upside down in so many ways. "If you're lying…"

He shrugged, like a man who spoke the truth. "You know I'm not."

He was right. Without another word I walked out of his bedroom door. I didn't give a fuck who tried to stop me. When I reached the bottom stairs a guard stepped out of a side room. He paused when he saw me then drew his gun.

"Let him pass." Liu's voice came from behind me.

I kept moving and opened the front door. I paused on the threshold. "I'm sorry about Jai."

"He made his choice. He backed the wrong side. As did the others."

I nodded and walked into the night to confront the real demon in this nightmare of my life. My world crumbled around my feet but only one thing like a beacon in my mind remained. Kept me sane. Kept me from roaring into the night. Ivy. She was all that mattered. I had to find her and she damn well better be alive.

I jumped into the car but this time I sat in the front seat.

"What happened?" Will asked. "Do I need to send in a cleanup detail?"

I turned my head to look at him. My hand already set to grab my blade if I needed to. "Who do you work for, Will?"

He frowned. "You."

"Who hired you?"

"The contract with me is through the Tong. But your stepfather hired me to protect Tsang and you. I was told if anything ever happened to Joe you were to become my priority. So since his death I've been working for you, along with Mark, twenty-four seven."

"And Tsang?"

"He's got his own security detail. So far he's never tried to pull me off your watch," he said.

"If he did?"

Will looked right at me. "He'd have to pass that through you first. If you assigned me to him then I'd go. But that's up to you."

Nothing about him indicated anything but that he spoke the truth. And he'd helped me tonight. I breathed a sigh of relief. "Okay. Don't worry about what went down in there. No clean up necessary."

He raised his eyebrows at me. I could tell he was curious as hell but Will didn't ask unnecessary questions. I gave him the address to the warehouse I'd just memorized.

"Is that where Ivy was taken?" he asked.

"I believe so."

"I think I've been there before with Mr. Tsang. Not sure. I'll know when I see the place."

I tucked the additional information away as we sped through traffic. It didn't take long for us to arrive.

"There's a blind alley where we can park," Will said. "There are three entrances into the place, but the best way in is still the front door. The other entrances have bars across them."

We pulled into the alley and Will cut the engine. "If you jump the wall it will put you right into the parking lot perpendicular to the warehouse lot. Go around the side. There could be a lookout at the front but people come in and out of the area all the time at all hours. A lot of retailers use this place to receive their deliveries or to hold them until they can be moved so trucks and foot traffic isn't that uncommon. There might be someone outside at the main entrance to keep an eye out for signs of trouble. If you can get close to him, you can take him out and gain entrance to the building."

I turned to look at Will. "Thank you. Why are you helping me?"

"Joe. He saved my life."

I studied Will. He was maybe mid-forties but looked younger than his real age. There was something about the way he walked and moved and the lines around his eyes. "You were a fighter."

"A long time ago, and Joe got me out."

"Did he train you?"

"Yeah, for a while, but I got into trouble. I was supposed to throw a fight. Joe saw to it I didn't have to fight. He got me on a flight out of China that night. He's kept in touch with me over the years. Helped me set up this company and I have done jobs for him from time to time."

"That sounds like him."

"He was a good guy."

I nodded then got out of the car and closed the door. I

made my way over the wall. I stopped to pull up the hood on the black sweatshirt I wore to obscure my features and then put on tight black gloves. I kept my hands at my sides visible, harmless. Like I was just stretching my legs. My appearance was ready now just in case a guard stood outside. I strolled around the building. And yep, I spotted a lookout ten feet away from me, leaning against the wall beside the door.

"Yo man," I said, and moved closer, still keeping my head down and staying within the shadows. "You got a spare cigarette?"

The guy had a cigarette in one hand. The other had moved to the inside of his jacket at my approach. "No, man. Keep the fuck moving."

I held up my hands. "No, worries. Chill."

I lowered my hands, and as I did, I slipped the knife I'd placed up my sleeve into my palm. Between one inhale of his cigarette and the next, I threw the knife and it buried in the side of his neck.

I rushed forward to grab him, then lowered him to the ground. I took out my knife and wiped it clean on his sweatshirt then grabbed the gun he had in the inside pocket of his jacket. I transferred it to the back of my waistband.

I placed my ear to the door he guarded, trying to hear

any movement on the other side. I decided to brazen it out. I pulled the gun out from behind me and gripped the doorknob. I turned it and pushed the door open, gun straight out and ready to meet any threat.

I walked into what appeared to be a small waiting area. There were three chairs on my right and a counter in front of me. I saw a hallway and doors, possibly offices, on the other side of the counter. The sound of faint voices came from behind the first door on the left.

Quietly, I closed the door behind me and made my way around the counter into the hallway. The first door wasn't closed all the way and I looked through the cracks of the opening. It was some sort of kitchen. Two men sat at a round table, both wore gun straps.

I found the right place.

I preferred to take the men out without the use of firepower. I wasn't sure how many others were in there and I didn't want to take any chances with Ivy's life. I needed to draw them out. Carefully I moved slightly away from the partially open door and went back to the reception area, looking for something I could use. I spotted a stress ball on a shelf and grabbed it.

Staying against the wall and away from the open portion of the door, I threw the ball away from me. It bounced, making a soft thudding noise. I drew my blades, crouched on the other side of the door and waited.

I didn't have to wait for long.

I heard the sound of both men pushing the chairs back and then footsteps. Guns drawn in their hands, they opened the door wider.

Too bad for them.

Their focus was in the direction the noise had come from. The minute the first one stepped through the door, I pinched the nerve in his gun hand and then stabbed him in the chest. Before the guy behind him could decide to squeeze off a round, I threw a blade between his eyes. Both men hit the floor at the same time.

I removed my knives, cleaned off the blades, and afterward I dragged them into the room where they'd been sitting. Closing the door behind me. I took their guns before continuing down the hallway before me, carefully checking the other two doors on that level. I turned right at the end of the hall that led to another longer one.

At the end of it I saw stairs leading down and another door with a bar over it. But midway, there were two more doors.

I listened again at both doors and heard nothing. The first door was unlocked, and I pushed it open slowly but it was just a room full of boxes lined against the opposite wall. No one was in there. I tried the other door. It was locked.

Chapter Seventeen

Ivy

I don't know how much time had passed. My foot was numb from sitting in this position so long on the hard floor. I got the boot off and that helped a lot, but the rest of my body was sore and my face throbbed. I felt it swelling. At least nothing was broken. The whole experience could have been worse. It still could.

I stood, walking around to get a little circulation going, when I heard someone at the door. I froze and stared at the knob, expecting one of my captors to come through the door. Which one, I didn't know.

My heart beat hard against my chest as I watched the knob turn but the door didn't open. That was odd. Whoever came in here had a key to get in. I walked over to the door and rested my ear against it. Yes, I heard footsteps.

"Hello?" I called tentatively.

"Ivy?"

"Oh, God, Maze! Maze! Is that really you?" I banged on the door. "Here. I'm in here."

"Hang on, baby. I'll be right back."

"No! Please don't leave me."

"Ah, fuck! Okay, just stay calm and move as far away from the door as you can."

I hurried to the other side of the room, and put my boot back on, my heart racing.

"I'm clear," I yelled, hoping he could hear me.

I jumped when I heard the sound of a gunshot, then pounding before the door slammed back.

Tears poured down my face. "Maze. Maze."

That's all I seemed capable of saying as he came into the room and sprinted to me. As soon as he touched me, my legs gave out, and I fell to the floor, taking him down with me.

"Oh, Jesus, Ivy. Oh, Jesus." They were the only words Maze seemed able to say.

I wrapped my arms around his neck and sobbed into his shoulder. I felt myself being lifted but I didn't care because I was in his arms. I was safe. I knew he'd come for me.

He kept a hand over my head like he didn't want me to move. I wasn't planning on it.

"We need to get out of here now."

I finally glanced up at the sound of a familiar voice.

"Will?" He stood framed in the doorway a gun in his hand. I was almost as glad to see him as I was Maze.

"Come on you two. Let's get out of here. There might be more guards."

"Three men were in the car when I was grabbed," I said.

"Okay," Will replied. Maze still hadn't said a word. He seemed to be in shock. I stroked his face and he leaned into my caress.

"Let's go, Will," he finally spoke.

We walked down a hallway turned a corner then down another longer hallway before we came to a counter that separated a reception area. Maze followed Will as he maneuvered around it. He opened a door and we were outside. The car was right in front of the entrance. As Maze put me in the car, I noticed the body slumped on the ground near the entrance. I recognized the blue denim jacket of the man in the backseat and who'd tried to rape me. It's easy to abhor violence in principal and from a distance. But when you're forced into it, with no chance of evasion, running away, or talking yourself out of it, it's funny how that changes. It was the son of a bitch who'd tried to rape me. I hoped he rotted in hell. Maze got in beside me and wrapped me in his arms. I felt a slight pang for the man who'd stopped the rapist, but I knew I was just bait to lure Maze. I couldn't forget that.

"Home, Will," Maze said.

"Do I need to do a quick clean up first?"

Maze raised one hand to show he wore gloves. "Taken care of."

I didn't understand what they were talking about and didn't care. I felt the car moving and Maze's warmth surrounding me.

"I'm so fucking sorry," he breathed into my hair.

I raised my head to look at him and saw the tears sliding down his cheeks. I was shocked, my Maze crying. That was all wrong. "No, Maze. You saved me. You saved me."

"It was because of me this shit happened to begin with. I thought sending you away…distancing myself from you would protect you. It didn't. Instead, it left you vulnerable. I should have kept you fucking glued to my side."

I sighed. "I can't let you blame yourself for this. You're not the one who did anything wrong."

He gently touched my face and I flinched. "Sorry. I can see you're hurt. Where else do you hurt, baby? What else did they do to you? Do you need a doctor?"

I felt the vibration of his heart as it hammered against his chest. The floor lighting provided enough illumination for me to see the fear in his eyes and I understood what he really wanted to know. I shook my head. "They just slapped me around a little, but…I'm fine. I promise. I will be okay as long as I'm with you."

"Are you sure? Swear it."

"I swear it."

He lowered his head to kiss me but the minute his lips touched mine fire rushed through my mouth and not the good kind. "Ouch."

"Shit. I'm sorry." He brushed my hair back from my face.

"No, no it's fine. I'm just a little beat up."

"So I see. Shit. I can't look at you and not hurt, too."

I raised my hand and wiped the tears off his face. "I'll heal and we're fine."

He pulled me onto his lap and we sat there with our arms wrapped around each other. Finally, I pulled back a little. "There were three men who took me, Maze. I saw the one by the door but not the other two."

I shivered in his arms in spite of knowing I was safe with Maze. Those men wouldn't be able to take me from him.

"You don't need to fear them ever again."

"Are they dead?"

At first he didn't say anything then he turned his head and stared out the window. I watched him so I saw the slight nod of his head. I didn't say anything else. I just enclosed my arms tighter around him and placed my head on his shoulder.

"Is it over?" I asked.

He hesitated. His hand however caressed my back, up and down in a soothing motion. "Before day break it will be."

"What does that mean?"

"There's one more."

We pulled up in front of the gym. Mark waited at the door for us. Maze got out of the car and so did Will. Both looked up and down the street, then Maze bent back to take my hand and help me out of the car. I only stood for a nano-second before he put his arms under my legs. He straightened and he picked me up. I loved his strength.

Mark unlocked the door for us and followed us upstairs. Will stayed with the car. Maze unlocked our door. We went into the apartment but Mark remained outside. Maze locked the door and took me straight to our bedroom. After he placed me on the bed he went into the bathroom. I heard the water running into the tub. After a few minutes, he returned to me and again picked me up and took me to the bathroom. He undressed me. I glanced at myself in the wall mirror over the duel sinks. I didn't realize there'd be bruises on my body, too. I looked like I'd been in a fight. Which I had. Maze gently placed a kiss on each one of those purple spots. He picked me up and placed me in the tub of warm water.

My aching limbs relaxed into the heavenly embrace of the soothing liquid. Maze got a washcloth, and sitting on the edge of the tub, he washed me from head to toe. Being careful around my cut lip and the bruise on my cheek.

When he was done, he took me out and dried me. I was docile the entire time. I could have bathed myself, but I understood he needed to do this for me. And well, I needed him to take care of me. It's what people do when they love someone and almost lost them. He opened the medicine cabinet and took out four Ibuprofens. I took them from him and swallowed them, taking a sip of water from the faucet. He folded a towel around me, then picking me up, carried me to the bed. After he put me down, he rummaged around in one of his drawers until he found a t-shirt. As if I were a child, he dressed me. And again I let him.

He pulled the covers back. "Get in," he said.

I did. He straightened the covers, pulling them up to my chin. He sat on the bed and kissed each eyelid. "Go to sleep and this will all be over when you wake up."

He started to get up, but I grabbed his wrist.

"Wait. Aren't you staying with me? Where are you

going?"

He sat back down on the bed. "To finish this, once and for all, Ivy. I could have lost you tonight. I'm making sure you are never ever going to be in danger again. This shit ends now."

I felt my lips trembling along with my body. "What…what are you going to do?"

He leaned forward and kissed my forehead. "I'm going to cut off the head of a snake."

Then he stood up. "Mark will remain right outside the door and Will can stay downstairs."

"You're not taking them with you? At least take Will."

"No. This is something I have to do alone."

"What if I don't want you to go? What if I ask you to stay?"

He took a deep breath. I saw a myriad of emotions cross his beautiful features. "Don't."

"But…"

"We'd never be safe, Ivy. You'd never be safe. The only other way would be for you to really leave me. Or for me to leave and turn over everything Joe worked for most of his life to the Triad. Put others at risk. Cause it's not just your life at stake here or mine. But all the people Joe also protected."

I cried at his words. I didn't understand all of it but I knew these people were ruthless. I'd experienced that first hand. They wanted Maze dead and they'd used me tonight to hurt him. If I could have left him I would. God help me I would, but I couldn't nor could I let him leave me.

"Goddamnit, Maze, you make damn sure you come back to me."

He smiled. "I'll be here when you wake up."

Chapter Eighteen

Maze

It broke my heart to see my baby's face bruised. They hurt her. I wanted to kill those fuckers again. This time with my fucking hands. Slow. I couldn't believe I'd cried like a baby in the car, but damn it hurt to see her like that. I will NEVER let anything harm her again. As long as I live and even in death I'd come back to kill any sonofabitch who threatened her. I had one final task to complete before I could rest easy at my lady's side. And this hurt like a bitch, too.

The depth of my uncle's betrayal.

I found it hard to fathom. This was someone who was almost as close to me as Joe. My earliest memories are of Joe and me, but riding a hot second are memories involving my uncle Tsang, pulling me down the street in a red wagon. When I was old enough and ready, he even gave me my first real blade. He was one of my first trainers besides Joe.

When I came out of the building, I saw Will step out of

the shadows and cross the street toward me. He must have been watching the entrance. I didn't alert him I was leaving the building.

"Going somewhere?" he asked coming to stand in front of me.

"Yes. But I need you to stay here and watch over Ivy."

He looked down at the ground then back at me. "You sure?"

"Yeah."

"You know I should try harder to stop you."

I smiled. "You and I both know you can't."

Will grimaced. "Good point. Just be careful."

I nodded at him. He knew exactly where I was going and who I would have to face. I pulled my hood up, and took out my phone to text Dante. I just let him know Ivy was home safe and she'd call him in the morning.

I put my phone away and stuck my hands back in my pockets as I walked the five blocks. Uncle Tsang had the corner row house. When I got there I was surprised to find no spotters around the property. I knocked on the door and Jason, one of Tsang's guards, opened it.

"He's downstairs," Jason said.

I walked farther into the room and heard the door close behind me. I glanced around, but the guy had left. I paused for a moment, allowing my senses to get a feel of the house. I didn't think there was anyone else there. He had no kids and his wife spent more time in Hong Kong than here. At least none of Tsang's guards were immediately visible.

I made my way to the elevator in the hall. I'd been to this house many times before we left for Japan, and even after Joe and I returned to the U.S. Tsang visited us too in Japan and all over Asia. Wherever we were, we saw him a few times a year. He was always present at my major fights. I'd learned a lot from him. I stepped onto the elevator and took it down to the lower level. He had a gym down there. I knew that's where I'd find him.

The elevator stopped, I stepped off and immediately saw him. He sat in the lotus position in the center of the exercise floorboards. The light overhead shone off his baldhead and the short blade resting across his lap.

I took off my sweatshirt, dropping it on the carpet beside me. I pulled the blade I'd taken from my apartment out of the strap I wore at my back. It was the first steel I'd ever owned. Mate to the one in front of me. Unsnapping the holder, I let it fall to the floor. I approached the wooden mat and stood at the edge. And waited. His eyes were closed but he knew I was there. Slowly and finally, he opened his eyes. Resignation seemed to lay in his gaze as he stared at me.

He sighed. "I did not want it to be like this. I loved Joe like a brother and you as a son. Do you know you are my heir to everything? I never wanted you dead. The assassins were merely a final test."

"No, you just wanted to kill everyone I loved. The next time you close your eyes will be your last. This ends now."

"All I ever wanted was to be Dragon Master and for you to stand at my side as enforcer, as I stood beside Joe. I let Joe establish the Tong, encouraged it, but he left everything to you. All of it. I was fine with that, as long as I had the Triad but I needed a few things out of the way first. Joe and Liu."

He stood and withdrew the blade from its sheath, tossing the casing aside. "I was going to return Ivy to you. I thought you'd have gone after Liu and killed him after you found her. But you did it backwards. Didn't wait for me to bring Ivy to you. I knew once you had her back you'd go after Liu, and you'd be able to get past his security. But you went to him first and left him alive. That's when I knew he told you everything. By the time I found out you'd already gotten Ivy. So I've just been waiting for you."

I was done listening to him. I did not know this man. I'm not sure I ever did. "Joe trusted you. Loved you and you betrayed him. For that alone I will kill you."

I stepped onto the floor and he came at me. This was not a fight like any I've ever fought. This time I not only fought my mentor, an enforcer, someone who trained me and knew my weaknesses, but also someone I trusted and loved.

I shoved all that aside as I'd been trained to do. I stored those emotions in a little box and sealed it shut to deal with later. For now my sole focus was on stopping the ache in my heart. The only way to do that was for him to stop breathing. Best to get this over with quickly.

Tsang spun and lashed out with his blade at the same time, catching me across the bicep. My mind registered the cut but blocked out the pain, rejecting the numbness.

I followed him immediately, mirroring his turns without missing a beat. I caught him in the heart when he came out of his motion, driving the sword deep enough there would be only one outcome. He lowered his arms and shock transformed his features. He looked down at the blade and then back up at me, recognition in his gaze. He nodded once, rubbed the hilt before firmly grasping his hands around it and shoved it in deeper, falling to his knees in front of me.

I breathed a sigh of relief. It was over. Now all I had to do was live with the blood on my hands. But Ivy was safe. I'd never have to fear for her life again. I turned around but my body remained numb. All I could think of was getting to

Ivy. I stepped on the elevator and went back to the main floor. I found Will in the living room waiting for me.

"Do I need to clean up?"

"What?" I was in a daze but recognized Will's voice. I knew he'd asked me that question before tonight and each time the answer had been no. But for some reason I couldn't answer it this time.

"Go, get in the car," he ordered. "It's right out front. I'll be there in a few minutes. Go."

I nodded my head and opened the door before walking out. I made my way down the stairs and found the car double-parked on the street. I got into the front seat, closed my eyes and waited. I don't know how long he took. Time seemed to stop for me. Something inside of me had died tonight. The radio was on and an Evanescence song came on, the words resonated in my soul. I felt dead inside. I needed Ivy to breathe life back into me. I only had to hang on a little while longer. Keep the darkness at bay until I could just hold her one more time.

The car door opened and Will got in. "You okay?"

"Take me home, Will. I want to go home."

"Hang on. Here." He handed me my sweatshirt that I'd dropped on the floor. I took it from him and just held it on my thigh.

"And everything is going to be fine," he said. "I took care of things in there. You're clear."

I heard his words but I was too tired to try to ferret out his meaning. I closed my eyes. When I opened them again the car was parked in front of the gym.

"One last thing," Will said before I could let myself out of the car. I turned to look at him.

"What?"

"You'll probably be questioned by the cops, at least to notify you about Tsang's death. Tell them you were at the club but left early and came back here. That you were working out almost all night with Mark and me. That's the pattern you've had for the last couple of weeks and easily verified by others."

"What?"

"You heard me. Understand."

I nodded. I did. "Thank you. And thank you for following me."

I let myself out and unlocked the outer door. I took the steps two at a time. Mark still stood in front of our door just as I'd left him.

"You can go," I told him and unlocked the door. I stopped in front of the closet with the washing machine and dryer. Looking down at myself, I was a mess. You couldn't see the blood against the black of my shirt but I could see the spots. I opened the door and stripped, even taking off my underwear. I kicked off my boots and took off my socks, then stuck them all in the washing machine. I put soap in and turned it on. I shut the door.

Naked, I walked into our bedroom, but I made it a point to keep my gaze down and not to look toward the bed. I didn't want to see or go to Ivy until I was clean. Or at least as clean as I could get my skin.

I went to the bathroom. I turned on the shower and stepped into the stall, letting the hot water wash over me. I put my head under the water, my hands rested against the wall. I watched blood go down the drain and I couldn't tell you if the water falling on my face came from the faucet or my eyes. I heard the soft click of the door opening that I'd closed.

Still, I didn't lift my head. Not until I felt small soft hands on my back. They moved to encircle my waist and she plastered her tits against my back and held me tight.

"You should be asleep," I told her.

"It's my turn to take care of you now." Ivy turned me around until I faced her and then placed her hands around my neck pulling my face down to her. She placed her mouth over mine and her tongue invaded my mouth.

I moaned, inhaling her deeply. I could breathe again. I tightened my grip on her waist and plastered our bodies even closer together. I guided her backward, pressing her against the tiled wall. I flexed my legs and grabbed her thighs, lifting her. She wrapped her legs around my waist. Her hands wound around my neck, and I raised her higher until we were perfectly aligned.

I felt between our bodies. Grabbing my cock, I eased inside her. She felt incredible. I sighed and bent my knees so I could push into her even more. She used gravity to bear down on me, taking me deeper inside her. I began to move, and with each stroke, her muscles clenched me, firing my blood, letting me know I was alive. I wasn't going to last long so I increased my pace. I moved one hand so I could rub my thumb against her clit.

"Come for me, babe. Milk my dick. Come, then make me come. Take all of me."

"Oh God, Maze. Oh God."

She shook in my arms. Her muscles contracted both inside and out and that's all I needed to trigger my own eruption into her waiting haven. My legs trembled. I lowered her legs so she could stand, and I rested my head back against the wall, still holding onto her waist. In truth, she and the wall were what held me up.

She kissed my shoulder. "I love you."

I raised my head and moved the hair out of her face and placed it behind her ears. "You are my everything. I love you."

We finished showering and toweled each other dry. She opened up a cabinet and found the first aid kit. I didn't say anything as she took a large pre-medicated Band-Aid out then placed it over my cut. She kissed it when she was done. I picked her up, and naked, I took her back to bed. After laying her down, I turned her on her side so she rested with her back to me and I held her close against my body. I slid my arm around her waist and rested my leg between hers. She pressed back against me and took a hold of my hand.

"Sleep, babe," she said. "Sleep."

I wasn't sure what tomorrow would hold for us. But as long as we faced it together I wasn't going to give a shit. I would bring her no more harm.

Chapter Nineteen

Ivy

I heard the door open and Maze entered the outer room. I thought he'd come straight into the bedroom but he didn't. Then I heard the washing machine going and I understood he must have turned it on. I wondered why he'd want to do laundry at dawn. I heard him in the hall near our door and relaxed back under the cover. I pretended I was sleeping but I saw when he stepped into the room—naked. When he went straight to the bathroom and shut the door, I sat up. My mind ran through all kinds of scenarios. None of them good. I heard the shower go on and I got out of bed. I had to know, had to be sure he was all right. He'd taken care of me earlier. I couldn't help but feel he needed me now. I opened the bathroom door as quietly as possible and pulled the t-shirt I wore off, dropping it to the floor. I opened the shower stall and stepped in.

I turned him into my arms, drinking in the sight of him. I noticed the cut on his arm, it wasn't very deep and the water had washed off most of the blood. Other than that there were no new marks on him. I breathed a sigh of relief. He was fine. Without a word we took care of each other. He needed the closeness and comfort I knew only I could give him as he gave me. And that's what we did.

Afterward when we went back to bed. He held me in his arms and I pretended to sleep. I felt his body relax and his breathing even out. My Maze slept and I was glad he rested safe and sound, home with me.

My mind wanted to shy away from what happened to me earlier tonight and what I suspected Maze did to save me, what I knew he did even afterward to keep me safe, but I found letting it go was hard. I asked God for forgiveness and prayed we'd make it through this. The only thing I needed to decide, really, was if I wanted him to tell me the details. If I should ask or just let him tell me if he chose. I decided this was not something I could ask him and demand the details. I could give him that. I knew tonight whatever he had to do affected him. I refused to let it affect our relationship. His actions stemmed from love and a need to protect me. A weight lifted off my shoulders. I'd made my decision. The only one I could make. I would not press him.

I awoke the next morning to the sensation of being surrounded and aroused by the man I love. He suckled at my breast and his fingers stroked against my clit. My sex immediately readied for him. I was wet. He slipped a finger inside me.

"Mmm," I murmured and opened my eyes to look into the storm filled gray of his.

"Good morning," he said. A grin on his face.

I entwined my arms around his neck. "I'll say."

"How are you feeling?"

"Perfect. You?"

He smiled. "The same."

"Is it…" I had to know. "Is it over?"

"Yes." He lowered his face to mine and kissed me. At the same time he removed his hand and eased himself inside me. Flicking my clit at the same time, causing my inner muscles to spasm. I raised my legs and crossed them over his waist. He shifted and pushed even deeper into me until I felt his balls rubbing against my lower lips. He pulsed inside me, and I shuddered as heat built in my core. With each stroke, he took me higher onto the summit until I stood at the top and fell over the side. He didn't give me pause, but picked me up and took me to the heights again. He moved faster and I kept his pace. He took me to the edge and together we dove over that cliff. He grasped my hands in his as he came and squeezed our fingers together.

"Never leave me, Ivy. Never."

"I won't."

We spent the entire morning making love, never leaving the bedroom. We ignored the buzzing of both our phones. It was as though we needed to make sure the other was fine.

My face would be a mess for a few days, and that slice on his arm needed another Band-Aid. He'd rubbed some salve on my face and I put a Band- Aid on his arm. Other than the one bathroom run to take care of those things, we hadn't left the bed. About midday my stomach rumbled.

Maze laughed then placed a kiss on my belly. "I think someone needs some food."

"I guess someone burned up all the fuel I'd previously stored."

He rolled away from me and grabbed his cell. He read it for a minute. "You better check your phone and call Dante so he doesn't come over here. He left me five texts and three phone messages. I'm going to call Will and have him go get us some breakfast."

"You're right I better call him. What…what should I tell him?"

He sighed. "The less the better for him. Tell him you're fine and we're taking a few days to spend together. In fact, I like that idea. We're taking a vacation. But we're not leaving this room. I'll have Will make a grocery run so we don't have to get take out every day."

I smiled, liking the idea of taking a vacation at home. Enclosed with him, protected from the rest of the world. "I'm not sure it's part of a bodyguard's description to make grocery store runs."

Maze laughed and it reached his eyes. I was glad. I never wanted to see the kind of despair I saw in them last night.

I sat up, grabbed my phone, and called Dante. He was happy I was all right and to hear from me. But he was understandably angry at my vague description about why I'd disappeared. I explained to him I just needed some time to think and went off by myself for a while. I told him Maze and I had worked things out. I wanted to spend a few days with Maze, so Dante and I had to put off training for a week. I figured by then my face would have cleared up enough I could be around Dante without him asking even more questions, or worse, think Maze hurt me. I shuddered to think what would happen then. I knew Dante cared about me and God alone knew what he'd try to do to Maze and what Maze would do to him.

I hung up the phone. Maze lay back on the bed and rubbed his fingers up and down my arm. I'd heard him call Will and tell him what we needed.

"Everything go okay?" he asked.

"Yes. Dante naturally wants to know what happened. Not sure he believed me when I said I just wanted a little time to myself. But he accepted it."

He nodded. "It's for the best."

"I know. I just hated lying to my friend. I'm not exactly sure what I was lying about."

Crap. I didn't want to challenge him in any way as to what happened last night.

He leaned forward and kissed my shoulder, then placed his arm over his face. "Trust me it's best that you don't."

He lowered his arm and looked at me. I lay down and turned on my side. He turned to face me and placed his hand on my hip. I put mine on his chest. There was something else going on here. I could still sense an underlying sadness inside him.

"What's wrong?"

"I won't tell you what happened last night. Not all of it but I do need to let you know something. The Triad. Uncle Tsang was behind it all. I need to stop thinking of him as my adoptive uncle. He wasn't exactly what he appeared to be."

"I don't understand. What are you talking about?"

He sighed. "Tsang had Joe killed. He's the one who had

you abducted."

I sat up again. "What!"

"I don't understand it all myself but it goes far back into Tsang and Joe's history. Tsang wanted more than he had and Joe stood in his way."

"And you."

"Oh me, he wanted to stand at his side. He thought the only way to do that was to take away from me the people I loved. He let me think someone else was behind it all. But all this time it was Tsang. Always Tsang."

"Oh, Maze. I'm so sorry." I rested my head on his stomach and just held him. He stroked my hair. I felt the gentle rise and fall of his chest.

"After Joe, he was the closest thing to family to me. Some family, huh?"

I raised my head. "Not everyone is like that."

"I know. I know your family isn't. I've seen the closeness you all share."

"Yes, and you're now a part of it because you're a part of me. Never forget that. I love you. You will always have me. Always be able to trust in us."

He smiled but there was still a hint of sadness there. It might be a long time before it was gone completely, but I'd do my best to make damn sure of it.

There was a knock on the door. Maze got out of bed and put on a pair of shorts. He left the bedroom and a minute later, I heard him talking to Will so I took the opportunity to run to the bathroom.

I put Maze's robe on since mine was at Dante's condo. Crap, I wouldn't be able to get my stuff back until next week and some of my favorite pieces of clothing were there. Oh, well. I suspected I wouldn't need much anyway.

I went into the kitchen and found Maze fixing us both a cup of tea. He'd already spread the bagels out on plates for us. He turned around when I entered and put the cups he held in his hands on the breakfast table. I limped over to him and kissed him.

"How's your foot?"

"It's fine. I wanted a break from the walking cast so I'm just babying it."

He pulled out my chair for me, and I smiled before sitting down. He waited until I was seated before taking his place. I grabbed my bagel and took a big bite. It was delicious.

"I thought we'd talk about what we wanted from the grocery, and I was going to send Will or Mark a text with a list of the stuff to pick up."

"That's a good idea," I agreed.

"And I'll even cook for us tonight."

I smiled. Who would have ever thought that day we met on the beach so long ago we'd end up here? The guy with the dragon tattoo down his side who got into fights at the drop of a hat would be willing to learn to cook for me.

"Did you ever think we'd end up here?" I asked.

He chewed and swallowed before answering. "I wanted this. I wanted this more than anything, but didn't dare even dream it."

"I did."

He smirked. "I know. I counted on that. And I'm going to do everything in my power to make sure all of your wishes come true."

Later that day, Maze got a call. We were putting away the groceries and he was trying to decide what to make for dinner when he answered it. "It's Will. I need you to go into the back bedroom and stay there."

"What's going on?"

"Some cops are on their way here and need to talk to me."

"What? No."

He grabbed my arm and hugged me. "Listen. I don't want them to see you. You have nothing to do with any of this. But, I need you to stay out of sight. If they don't see you then they have no cause to even think you were involved in anything that happened last night." He released me then opened up the dyer, he took out sweats and a t-shirt and quickly put them on. "Now, please, babe. Go to the back room and wait there for me. Go."

I felt tears welling in my eyes and knew he was right. One look at my face and there'd be questions. I wouldn't, couldn't, answer without doing Maze harm.

There was a knock on the door and I went to the backroom. I left the door slightly ajar and sat on the couch so I could try to hear what was said. I heard Maze open the door and the voices of two men. One identified himself as a detective. They came to tell Maze Tsang killed himself last night. It appeared to be a suicide. He'd stabbed himself with his own short sword. I almost gasped in shock but stopped myself before I uttered a sound. I thought Maze had killed the man.

I heard Maze tell them he'd seen Tsang a couple of days ago and he seemed fine. They wanted Maze to come down later this evening to identify the body. He agreed. They also asked him where he was yesterday. He told them he'd gone to a club and then come back home. That he'd been down in the gym working out until late. They wanted to know if he was with anyone. He gave them Will and Mark's names.

Then they left.

I stepped out of the room, but Maze was already headed in my direction. He gathered me into his arms and kissed me. I kissed him back. Giving him all of the passion he needed right then.

"Are you okay?" I asked.

"I will be. I have to go down to the morgue."

"Yeah, I heard. I know not all of that was true. But did Tsang really commit suicide?"

He stared at me a moment. "Do you really want to know, Ivy?"

"I…"

"He finished what I'd already begun."

"I don't understand, but it doesn't matter. I'll wait for you here."

He took a deep breath. "Hopefully, I won't be long."

"I'll be here. I'll even fix dinner."

He smiled sadly then went into our bedroom. I followed him and watched him change into jeans and gray sweatshirt. He sat on the bed to pull on his boots, then stood up and grabbed his keys and wallet from the dresser. He kissed me again as he moved past me toward the door. I blinked and he was gone. I felt sorry for my poor Maze. His uncle's betrayal cut deep. Family meant everything to him.

I don't know what compelled me to do it but suddenly I needed to talk to my mom, so I got my phone and called her. Besides, I had good news to tell her. When I'd spoken to Dante he told me RBA had chosen our piece as one of the ten performed at the festival. She was really excited about that. We spoke for awhile. Catching each other up. I hadn't spoken to her for about a week. She didn't know I'd moved back in with Dante and no need to tell her now. She told me Bev was doing great and would probably come to the festival, too. I'd love nothing more. Before we got off the phone she told me give Maze her love. I smiled when I hung up. My mom. She always knew what to say and when to say it. That's what Maze needed most now. Love. And I would show him he had plenty of it.

By the time Maze got back I had a couple of candles lit on the table and a bowl of mac and cheese, salad, and garlic bread laid out on the table. Everything came out of a box or a bag. Gourmet cook I'm not.

The front door opened and shut, then I heard Maze's voice. "Hey, honey. I'm home. And I see you've been slaving over a stove for me all evening."

"You know it." I'd actually called Mark and asked him to text me when the car pulled up so I could put everything out just before he came upstairs.

He grabbed me around the waist and stared into my eyes. "I love you." Then he kissed me.

"Love you too, babe. Did everything go all right?" I watched that hint of sadness creep back over his features.

"Yeah. It went fine. They're going to run some tests before they rule out a homicide. But they also know there's a gang war going on and suspect Tsang might be another causality."

"Oh, baby."

"It's fine. I'm not a suspect. Everyone knows how close Joe and Tsang were, and how close I was to both men. They actually want to put me in protective custody. I told them that's what my bodyguards are for. It's all good, babe."

I smiled and took his hand. I led him into the kitchen. "Sit, eat. This is comfort food. I thought we could both use some."

"This looks good, babe. Thank you. Tomorrow I'll cook."

"I'll hold you to it." I waited until he'd taken a bite. "Well, how is it?"

"It's good." He waited a beat then said. "From a box?" The smile on his face told me it didn't matter I didn't really cook. He loved it.

"I laughed. A package. By the way, I spoke to my mom

earlier. She told me to tell you she sends her love."

He choked and had to reach for the beer I'd placed on the table. I understood why he reacted that way. After everything he and I had both been through something as normal as my mother's love seemed out of place. But it was what he deserved and so much more.

"You all right?"

"Ah, yeah. Fine," he croaked out.

I took his hand and he held onto mine while we both continued to eat.

I believed with everything I was we would be fine.

Chapter Twenty

Maze

I stared out the window up at the evening sky. In the last six months Ivy and I had come so far and still had a ways to go. The coroner's report listed Tsang's death as a suicide because they couldn't find evidence to the contrary. The deaths of his men in the warehouse were attributed to a gang war and Tsang took his own life as a result of losing everything. I might have been his heir but there was more debt than funds. I knew his real wealth was tied up in the Triad and I wanted no part of it so whatever his share was they could keep. I'd already told Liu all of that.

I'd done everything I could to make sure I stayed out of it and kept Ivy out of all the shit. We were never apart for any significant length of time. Neither of us could really stand it. We'd both have anxiety attacks at times if we couldn't at least speak to each other. But we were getting better. Ivy could actually go to class and rehearsal for an entire day without me having to show up, or getting a text from Dante to get my ass down to the theater because she needed me. I wasn't really sure what happens next for us, but I knew whatever it was we'd be together.

Two things were happening tonight. Well, three. Ivy only knew about two. It was her return to dance. Her ankle was stronger than ever and tonight my girl was going to prove it to the world. Tonight, I was finally ready to take over as Dragon Master of the Tong. I would be its head in truth. I'd resisted for a long time, but I'd grown closer to the legitimate businessmen of Chinatown. They'd taught me a lot. And in my heart, I knew it was something I had to do and Joe would want. The Triad respected me. Funny what going on a killing spree will do for a rep. But this was also a way of making sure what Joe started so long ago would continue to prosper and remain free of corruption. The Triad was finished, at least as far as the Tong was concerned.

Ivy knew all about the Tong and that I'd been working with the legitimate businessmen in Chinatown. I finally fessed up and told her about my financial net worth. I laughed as I recalled the expression on her face. Her eyes had opened wide and her mouth formed a perfect O. Then she'd begun to cry. I had to make love to her to calm her down.

Tonight after I dropped Ivy off at her early cast call, I'd

head to the business headquarters of the association for a formal meeting. All the business leaders that made up the Tong would vote tonight to make me Dragon Master. The closest thing would be the CEO of a multi-faceted corporation. It was members only tonight, so Ivy couldn't go with me. She had to be at rehearsal before her performance anyway. After the vote, I would head over to Ivy's performance, and I'd meet her dad and Bev and Ben there. But before we left, there was one last thing I needed to do.

The sound of soft footfalls in our apartment coming up behind me made me smile. Slender arms wrapped around my waist. I took her hands and turned into her embrace. Bending my head, I captured her mouth and inhaled her. She opened for me, and I met her tongue with mine. For a while, we danced together, her and me. Our own private tango. Reluctantly, I withdrew and took a step away from her. I watched her and saw when she opened her eyes. They'd been closed while we kissed. She smiled. Then I dropped to both knees, while still holding her hand. I put one of mine in the pocket of my pants and pulled out the box I'd been carrying around for a while now. I kept my eyes on her so I saw the smile falter and her lips tremble. She raised her eyes to mine and I watched them fill with tears.

"Shhh, babe. Please, don't do that." I raised one hand

and wiped the moisture from her face. Then I took her hand again, and one handedly flipped the top of the box open with my thumb. I revealed to her the princess cut three-carat diamond ring on a platinum band nestled inside.

"I'm no poet. Far from it. But you manage to understand me anyway and still you love me. I'm not going to question that. Just make sure I keep you. My blood runs for you, my heart beats for you. I live only because you are in this world. I will love you like no other even after I die. All I ask is that you marry me, share a life with me, and let me love you all of our lives."

She was full out crying now. She tugged on my hand to pull me up and took the box from me. I enclosed my arms around her hips and smiled, waiting for her answer. She went up on her toes and kissed my cheek. "I love you so much, Maze. So much. But there is something I have to tell you first." She wiped the remaining tears off her face.

My heart slammed against my chest at those words. What could she have to possibly say before she said yes she'd marry me? "All I need to know is that you love me and say yes."

When she tried to tug out of my embrace that's when I knew something was wrong. I wasn't letting go and hung on tighter. "What the fuck is it, Ivy? Just tell me."

"You're going to have to stop cussing like that for one thing."

"Fine, whatever. Now, what's wrong?"

"Nothing's wrong. It's well. I'm pregnant."

I froze. Nothing moved, no synapses fired. I just froze. She stepped away from me.

It was only when I felt the lack of her warmth from her arms that I came out of my paralysis. Her mom stood at the door. I'd left it unlocked. I don't even remember hearing her knock or even the door opening. I'd forgotten she was coming with us to the theater. My brain synapses fired up again and I recalled; she wanted to be there early for the cast call with Ivy for support and to take some pictures.

"Hey, Maze," her mom said. She came over to me and kissed my cheek, giving me a hug as she did so. "You guys ready? I saw the limo downstairs. I hope I'm not too early."

That's right. She was catching a ride over with us in the limo. I'd drop her and Ivy off first then go to the meeting and return in time for the performance.

I automatically raised my arms and hugged her back. I was getting used to her hugs.

I straightened up and my gaze drifted over to Ivy. She picked up her dance bag she'd left by the chair. Fuck! She hadn't answered me and I hadn't responded to her. Shit. She had to know how much I loved her. How much I wanted our baby. Holy mother of God, she's pregnant! How the hell was I going to be a father?

"We better go, Maze. Maze."

Ivy spoke my name twice. I know I heard it, but my response time was way off. I shook my head trying to function. "Ah, yeah. The limo should already be in the front."

Wait I knew that already. We had a permanent reserved spot out front for the limo and Will knew to be there now and Allison said it was there. Still, I pulled out my phone and shot Will a text letting him know we were on our way down.

I walked over to Ivy. "Come on," I said, guiding her away by her elbow.

I couldn't say anything about what just happened with her mom right there. There was so much I wanted to say but it would have to wait when we were alone again, which would not be for several hours. I stifled a groan and circled my arm around her neck and pulled her to me.

"I love you," I whispered and kissed her temple. That's the best I could do for now. In truth, I was still a little shell shocked. I grabbed her bags away from her and we took the stairs so we didn't have to go through the gym. Will was right there on the sidewalk holding the door open for us.

Her mom got in first, then Ivy and me. All I could do was hold her hand and rub my thumb over the back of it. Soon enough we were at the theater and I got out to let Ivy and her mom out. I walked them to the side entrance, hoping I'd have a minute to speak to Ivy but it was not to be. Dante waited for her right at the door. I only had time to kiss her before she was whisked away from me.

She'd turned around and followed after Dante, when suddenly she stopped, tugged her hand out of his and ran back to me. She leaped and I opened my arms to catch her. She wrapped her legs around my waist and kissed me. I turned us in a circle and kissed her back. Letting it all out, letting her know how much she meant to me, and this life we'd created together and the future we would have. She pulled away and whispered, her breath brushing against my lips, one word, "Yes."

I put her down and placed my hand over her stomach. "Yes," I whispered back. "I want you both." Then Dante pulled her away again. I glanced up at him and witnessed his frown.

"Dude, you can do that later," he growled.

Laughing, Ivy blew me a kiss and followed after Dante. Her mom just grinned and winked at me. With a smile on my face, I went outside and got back into the limo. To implement the other part of my future, to ensure the one I had with Ivy would be like nothing that had gone down this year. I would become an official Dragon Master of the Tong. The war was over and I had won.

****

I got back to the theatre and took my seat minutes before the curtain rose. Was it less than a year ago I'd bought out this same box and sat by myself, watching the love of my life dance? Sitting here, ready to watch her performance took me back to the time I first saw her and how much she'd grown. The main differences are I love her even more today than I did that initial day and while I'd still bought out the entire box I didn't sit there alone. Her family, *our* family, sat with me along with Will and Mark. Her mom and dad sat on my left, Bev and Ben and the little five-year-old Cambodian girl they'd recently adopted sat at my right. Will and Mark sat behind us as guests, not guards, and Vin sat with them. The box was full this time.

Ivy and I had been through so much but we were stronger. No more threats on the horizon. We were in a solid place. Still, I took no chances. Will and Mark were both armed and I carried a blade strapped to my calf. I protected what's mine. I felt a hand on my shoulder and I looked at her mom.

"Did you ask her yet?" she whispered. But it was loud enough that everyone near us heard her and all eyes swung to me. Everyone there had known what I had planned. There were no secrets with this crowd.

I smirked, looking at all the grinning faces. "Yeah. I did."

"Well, don't keep us waiting," Bev said.

"She said yes."

"Oh my God!" her mom cried and so did Bev. Both women hugged me and the men shook my hand.

Whenever Ivy and I visited her folks in D.C. hugging me was something these two women had no trouble doing. They tried to mother everyone, even me. Ivy's family accepted and acknowledged my love for Ivy, our love for each other. I'd actually gone to see her parents the day before, when they'd first arrived in New York while Ivy was at a rehearsal. I asked them both for their blessing. That I was going to ask Ivy to marry me. I didn't ask their permission. We didn't need it. But I knew it would be important to Ivy to have their blessing. And they gave it. Her mom had cried and said, "Of course." Her dad in his gruff way said, "About time." But he and I got along fine. As long as I kept his little girl safe and happy he'd told me once, he was happy.

Was I going to have that kind of conversation with a boy some day? I had no idea how to be a father. Ivy would make a wonderful mother.

I didn't say anything about the baby. *Baby.* I still needed to wrap my mind around that one. But I'd let Ivy tell her parents. I knew she'd want to be the one to do that. I'm sure if I wasn't already marrying her, though, her father would have my head. I know I sure as shit would with any fuck who knocked up my daughter. Oh crap! We could have a girl. I'd have to get a new bodyguard just for her. To keep those little peckers away. I rubbed my hand over my face. Lord, I was in trouble. But life was good and would only get better for us.

The theatre went dark. The music started and I leaned forward in my seat. My eyes riveted to the stage. As I watched my pregnant fiancée dance, I raised my hand to my face once or twice during the performance. Of course, only to wipe away something that had gotten into my eye, but who could blame me.

After the show I'd rented a private room in a restaurant so we could have a celebration dinner. The place had live music and everyone was on the dance floor. I took my future into my arms and pulled her close. "If we have a daughter her name can be Shelly, and if a son, Sheldon. Either way we can call him or her Shel for short."

She raised her face to stare at me with tears in her eyes. "This. This is the reason I love you so. And always will no matter what. It's as simple as that."

"For me too, babe."

Epilogue

The cries of delight from a small child carried through the open window by the wind. Maze got up from the desk and walked out to the deck. He loved this house he'd bought right on the ocean. It had a gorgeous view. He loved the sight before him even more. They'd spend many summers here he thought, as he watched the little girl with the long wavy dark gold hair and honey-kissed skin doing these crazy ass leaps on the sand. He pulled out his Smartphone and took a few pictures. Then he walked down the steps onto the beach and approached the duo. The smaller replica of her mother mimicked her movements over the water.

The little girl looked up and spotted him walking toward them.

"Daddy," she squealed. She came running toward him, her little arms and legs pumping, and she took a flying leap right into his arms. Knowing he'd catch her. She laughed and wrapped her small arms around his neck. Her mother came over to them and kissed his cheek.

"There you are. It's about time you joined us," Ivy said.

"Who could work with all that noise?"

His wife's beautiful smile captured him all over again and it took him back. "Do you know, honey," he addressed their child, "That your mommy first met me on a beach very similar to this one? And she was doing those same leaps she just showed you."

"Ooohhh," the child said.

"Do you know what they're called?" he asked.

"Firebird," she yelled. "Put me down, Daddy. Lemme show you."

Maze put her down and she began to leap over the sand. It was like catching a brief glimpse from his past and he remembered.

The first time I saw her it was evening, that time of day when the setting sun hit the ocean and turned it a burnt orange. Most of the vacationers had deserted the beach for the restaurants, swarming the main drag or the barbecues in their rented backyards. There were only a few folks here or there walking or hanging around the water's edge.

She was doing these beautiful leaps into the air, but the one that stopped me in my tracks was the firebird. At the time I didn't know what any of them were called, only that the beauty of the evening paled in comparison to the female that stole my attention, as she propelled her body through the air. Like gravity had no hold on her.

Maze wrapped his arm around Ivy's waist. She wasn't quite showing yet but she was four months pregnant. "I think we have another little ballerina on our hands," he said, watching their daughter. "And if you keep dancing like that the little one in your tummy might turn out to be another dancer, also."

She smiled. "Would you mind?"

"How can I when I fell in love with a ballerina?"

"What if it's a boy?"

He paused then shrugged his shoulders. "I'll teach him to fight. In fact, I'll teach them both."

"Shelly," he called releasing his wife. "Come on and let's show Mom the exercises I taught you."

She came running over. This kid only had two speeds, off when she was asleep and fast the rest of the time. She got into a crouch beside him, mimicking his stance. Working in sync, she perfectly executed the kata he'd created.

About The Author

Ursula Sinclair is the alter ego for LaVerne Thompson, an award winning, best-selling, multi-published author, an avid reader and a writer of contemporary, fantasy, and sci/fi sensual romances. She writes romantic suspense and new adult under the pen name Ursula Sinclair.

She is currently working on several projects. Visit her website at http://lavernethompson.com to read excerpts of her books. Or join her on Facebook at http://facebook.com/groups/lavernesnews . On Twitter at http://twitter.com/lavernethompson

BOOKS BY LaVERNE THOMPSON

**Self-Published from Isisindc Publishing
Dragon's Heart- Story of the Brethren
The Ballerina & The Fighter- Book 1
Come To Me

**Horny Devil Publishing

Skye High

**From Decadent Publishing

Writing as Ursula Sinclair

White Wedding- The Guardian Agency Series Book 1

Something Blue- The Guardian Agency Series Book 2

Wine and Roses- The Guardian Agency Series Book 3

In print

Guardian Agents- All 3 books in The Guardian Agency Series

**From Phaze Books

Model Misbehavior

**From Freya's Bower

Believe

***Coming 2014/2015*

Sea Bride- Children of the Waves (re-release)

Sea Storm- Children of the Waves

Promises

Hold On

Ringside- Book 1 The Three Sisters Series

Masquerade- Book 3 The Three Sisters Series

Chances Are

Day in The Sun

Titanna

Living on The Edge

Kissed By A Rose

Highland Jack

Journey of the Princess of Ice- The Elementals

Lavernethompson.com

Some Great Authors I Read

Yvonne Nicholas- The Dragon Queen Series (Paranormal shapeshifters),

Victoria Smith- The Space Between, The Dividing Line (Contemporary multicultural new adult),

Sienna Mynx- Bad Habits, The Battaglia Mafia Series

(Multicultural romance),

Indigo Sin- Redeemed (The Passion Series) (Erotic romance),

Stephanie Williams- Cabin Fever (Menage-contemporary), Detention, Slave To Sensation (Erotic romance)

Ursula Sinclair